powerless

matthew cody
powerless

Alfred A. Knopf   New York

J
FIC
COD

Library of Congress Cataloging-in-Publication Data
Cody, Matthew.
Powerless / Matthew Cody. — 1st ed.
          p. cm.
Summary: Soon after moving to Noble's Green, Pennsylvania, twelve-year-old Daniel learns that his new friends have superpowers that they will lose when they turn thirteen, unless he can use his brain power to protect them.
ISBN 978-0-375-85595-5 (trade) — ISBN 978-0-375-95595-2 (lib. bdg.) —
ISBN 978-0-375-89353-7 (e-book)
[1. Supernatural—Fiction. 2. Bullies—Fiction. 3. Moving, Household—Fiction.
4. Schools—Fiction. 5. Family life—Pennsylvania—Fiction. 6. Pennsylvania—Fiction.
7. Mystery and detective stories.] I. Title.
PZ7.C654Pow 2009   [Fic]—dc22   2008040885

The text of this book is set in 12-point Hoefler New Roman.

Printed in the United States of America
October 2009
10 9 8 7 6 5 4 3 2 1
First Edition

To Faolan and Aedan, who gave me the inspiration to begin—
and to Alisha and Will, for giving me a reason to finish.

In loving memory of Shirley Ann Cody.

Prologue

The wind howled in Michael's ears. He would be picking bugs out of his hair for days, but he didn't care. The air down here was unusually warm for this time of year—an Indian summer. The heat and moisture had collected into a low-hanging cloud that hid the peak of Mount Noble, but it couldn't hide Eric and Mollie. He could just make out their silhouettes against the dark cloud-wall, and though he couldn't tell which was which, it was safe to assume that Mollie was out front. She was faster, the fastest flier Michael had ever seen. But then, speed wasn't everything.

He had given them a head start by counting to thirty before even leaving the ground. By now they were a good two hundred yards in the lead. Michael smiled to himself as he took in a deep breath of mountain air, savoring the clean tang of pine in his nostrils, and watched as the forest disappeared beneath his feet—this was going to be fun.

It wasn't enough to be naturally fast; you needed to know how to ride the wind if you wanted to win. If you fought too hard against nature, you would quickly tire and lose. So Michael held back until he found an updraft of warm air from the valley. Spreading his arms, he caught the wave of heat and added to it his own power, hurling himself straight up into the ceiling of gray cloud cover. Conditions were turning rough up here where the warm gusts met the cold, high winds, and soon the skies would be too dangerous to ride. Already Michael could feel his skin prickle with static, and it wouldn't take long for that static to turn to lightning.

But Michael would end this race long before that happened. Up and still farther up he soared, expending the last of the momentum borrowed from the updraft. In a great curving arc he flew, breaking the cloud ceiling for a glimpse of the twilight skies above, and then, folding his arms tight at his sides, he dove back down to earth like a rocket, like a meteor.

Cold rain stung his face as he plummeted through the mist, but he laughed anyway. He felt the speed in the pit of his stomach, in the tips of his fingers; he felt the speed in every nerve and it was exhilarating. When he cleared the clouds, he spotted Eric and Mollie, each a few hundred yards from the peak. They were looking over their shoulders, searching for him, confused by his sudden disappearance. But he wasn't behind them, he was above and in front, just seconds from the peak, just seconds from the chosen finish line.

He almost felt sorry for them, losing another race, their last race all together, but his pity didn't last long. It was swept away in the thrill of speed and freedom, drowned out by the roar of the wind. Michael was just born to fly. . . .

From the moment he opened his eyes, Michael felt as if something was wrong. It was a strange feeling, like waking up in a dark room in a bed that wasn't your own. But this was his bed—he recognized the sheets dotted with little stars and half-moons, and sunlight streamed through his open window, revealing blue sky outside. He was in his own room and he had woken to a beautiful early morning. And yet there was this nagging *itch,* somewhere in the back of his brain. Scratching at him, as if he'd forgotten or misplaced something.

Michael looked at the alarm clock next to his bed—*6:20 a.m.* Far too early for a lazy summer morning. Squeezing his eyes shut, he rolled over and tried to will himself back to sleep. But it was no good. He was wide-awake now, and after a few minutes of restless tossing and turning, he gave in with a sigh and hauled himself out of bed. Maybe if he got started with his day, he'd feel better.

Unsatisfied, the little itch in his head continued to scratch.

Michael grabbed a wrinkled pair of jeans off the floor and

the dirty T-shirt draped over the bedpost—he didn't feel like digging through his dresser for a clean one. When he had finished dressing, he looked in the mirror and gave himself a weak smile.

"Happy birthday, Me," he told himself.

He certainly didn't look thirteen. At least he didn't look the way he'd always pictured himself looking at such an important age. He'd always pictured the thirteen him as tall, more grown-up, maybe even with a muscle or two. But the boy in the mirror looked just as short and just as skinny. He looked, well, twelve.

As he frowned at the mirror, he noticed something odd. Something in the reflection that shouldn't be there. Once again he was in a room that he didn't quite recognize. It was something about the walls. . . .

When he turned around, he saw them everywhere. Drawings. They were taped to the wall above the bed, on the closet door, even stuck to the window. Everywhere he looked were more drawings—he must have been half blind not to notice them before. Leaning in close, he studied one. It was an ink sketch of a boy floating in a cloudy sky. Across the top, in bold Magic Marker, were the words "You Can Fly."

As he took a step back, he realized that they were all pictures of the same thing, repeated over and over again: the boy soaring above the rooftops or over the mountains or through the clouds. It was a little frightening. Though he couldn't remember drawing them, they looked like his—they all had the same awkward hands that he could never get right. And each one contained the same message written in his own messy scrawl:

You Can Fly.

Michael's first impulse was to call out for his parents. They were sleeping just down the hall, and if he yelled, they'd be there in a matter of seconds. But he was thirteen today, and thirteen was the age when you started taking care of yourself, when you started figuring things out, and so that was precisely what he decided to do.

Michael knew that when he was little, he would sometimes walk in his sleep. He'd wake up at the foot of his bed or at the other end of the hall. Once his parents had caught him at the front door. Perhaps he had gotten up in the middle of the night and drawn a bunch of pictures. He hadn't sleepwalked in years, but what other explanation was there?

Then something began to happen: the longer he stared at the drawings, the more they started to feel . . . familiar. The harder he concentrated, the stronger the feeling got. There *was* something about them that he recognized, beyond the badly drawn hands. It was like a memory of a dream—it didn't make sense exactly, yet it seemed so real. The itch in his head grew insistent and when he closed his eyes, he could almost hear the sound of wind roaring in his ears, feel the cold, crisp air biting against his cheek. . . .

All at once he felt sick. A queasy feeling twisted in his gut, and his head threatened to split open with a jabbing pain. His knees buckled as the room started to spin, and he had to grab hold of his desk just to stay upright. An awful fear gripped him—that there was something waiting for him when he closed his eyes. It was like a bad dream coming to life, a shadow blacker than the surrounding black—a living menace in the dark. And it was reaching for him, reaching . . .

And like that, it was gone. He opened his eyes and the darkness, the spinning, the horrible sickness—all of it vanished as quickly as it had come. The itch receded once more to the back of his brain, chased there by the terrible shadow.

"HAPPY BIRTHDAY, MICHAEL!"

He looked up to see his parents in the doorway. They were still in their pajamas.

"Hey, Michael, what's the matter?" asked his dad. "You look a little pale."

Michael thought about telling them everything that had just happened—the mysterious drawings, the strange memories of cold wind . . . the thing in the dark. They were his parents—surely they could help?

"I'm . . . I'm fine. It's just a little early in the morning," he answered instead. He was thirteen today, after all.

To Michael's parents his birthday party probably looked just like any other. The kids finished up their cake speckled with melted candle wax and went out into the yard to play catch. Eric teased Rohan whenever he dropped the ball (which was most of the time), while Mollie complained that boys didn't throw straight anyway, so why were they even playing such a stupid game? Louisa and little Rose just watched and cheered and tried to ignore Simon as he flicked ladybugs at their hair. But to Michael, everything felt different. He couldn't get those pictures out of his head, or the fear that if he shut his eyes for too long, something would be there waiting for him.

His friends were acting strange, too. On the outside they seemed all right—joking around and laughing—but Michael caught them giving each other looks when they thought he wasn't paying attention. It reminded him of when Charlie Campbell's dad passed away—how all the kids at school treated Charlie on his first day back. Everyone had been extra nice, but no one had been themselves.

When they got bored with playing catch, Michael half-heartedly asked what they wanted to do next. Rose pointed up at the sky and grabbed Michael's hand. "Let's go up! Let's go up!" she was saying.

Michael was about to ask Rose what she meant, but before he could say anything, Louisa shushed her sister and whispered something in her ear. For some reason Rose turned red-faced, ashamed. That was when Michael noticed how quiet it had turned. He looked around to see his friends all watching him, as if they were expecting him to burst into flames or something.

Michael didn't know why, but this made him absolutely furious. Why were they all staring at him anyway?

"Aren't you a little old to be picked up?" Michael snapped.

"What are you, Rose, some kind of baby?" He turned to the rest of his friends. "And why do you all keep staring at me? What's the matter with you?"

Louisa didn't look at Michael; she just put her arm around her sister and gently pulled her away. But Mollie turned and stalked off. Without a word, she got on her bike and pedaled away.

Michael looked around, confused. His head felt thick, as if it were stuffed with cotton balls. His eyes stung with tears. "What's going on?" he asked. "What'd I do?"

Eric took Michael by the shoulder, scowling as Mollie disappeared down the street.

"You didn't do anything, Michael. Mollie's just being a girl, you know?" he said, tossing him a catcher's mitt. "Here, wanna throw the ball around some more?"

But Michael didn't want to be outside anymore. He didn't want to be around *them* anymore. He dropped the mitt at Eric's feet and went inside without bothering to say goodbye.

After dinner he said good night early and went up to his room to be alone. He tried reading a comic, but it was just another story about some superhero doing impossible things, and that annoyed him, too. He found himself wondering why all those comics had to feature people doing crazy stuff, like lifting cars over their heads and outrunning trains. It was really pretty stupid when you thought about it.

Once again Michael studied the drawings on his wall. A

flying boy. It was as if someone had collected a montage of dreams and plastered his wall with them. A child's dreams.

He walked over to his desk and ripped the first picture down. The corners tore away, leaving four little triangles of paper and tape stuck to the wall. He ripped down another. Then another. It felt good. He was reaching for more when he saw something moving in the moonlight just outside his window. Michael's house was three stories tall, and his room was on the top floor. An oak tree grew outside his window, and the uppermost branches reached almost, but not quite, to the window. There, sitting in the tree, was Mollie. She was wearing a Windbreaker with the hood up, but he could still see her face. She looked upset, and she might even have been crying, but it was hard to see in the dark. As he watched, she slowly lifted from the branches of the giant oak until she was no longer in the tree but above it, several feet above the highest branches. And she was waving goodbye.

At that moment a cloud must have passed in front of the moon because the yard was suddenly covered in shadow, and Michael couldn't make out anything. He was so shocked that he couldn't even speak. He just stood there, frozen, waiting for the cloud to pass. When it did, Mollie was gone. All that was left was the old oak, swaying in the breeze.

Michael leaned heavily on his desk. He wanted so badly to give in to that itch—that dim memory somewhere in the corners of his mind—but the sickness threatened to return, and with it the shadow that haunted him. If he allowed himself to remember anything, he'd have to remember *everything,* and that was something he just didn't have the strength to do.

Michael suddenly surprised himself with a laugh—what an imagination he had, to think he saw Mollie out there floating in the yard! He had clearly spent too many hours reading too many comics and wasting his time with stupid drawings. Now he was seeing things—menacing shadows in his head and friends floating in trees. The sickness passed again with a few deep breaths, and this time the itch disappeared entirely and for good. His head clear for the first time all day, Michael gathered up the rest of his drawings and dumped them all, unceremoniously, into the garbage.

It was easy to forget now. A new voice in his head was whispering to him, telling him that it was time to put away childish things. He realized now that the voice had been trying to talk to him all day long, but he'd refused to hear it until now—that the itch had been keeping him too distracted. But no longer. He pulled the shade down, so he wouldn't be tempted to look out again at the old oak, and climbed into bed. He turned out the light, and before long he was fast asleep.

You Can Fly.

That night, and every night thereafter, Michael dreamt ordinary dreams.

You Can Fly.

And he never flew again.

Chapter One
The New Kid

The safest town on earth? thought Daniel. *Couldn't sound lamer.*

Daniel Corrigan and his family saw the sign from their car just a few miles outside town. When it came into view, Daniel's father honked the horn of their minivan as his mother clapped her hands. Of course Daniel's baby brother, Georgie, had to join in, squealing with delight while kicking his plump legs against his car seat. Georgie was only two years old and he always just assumed that everyone was clapping for him, which was usually the case. Daniel's parents clapped when Georgie smiled or spoke or even burped.

Instead of joining in the applause, Daniel just buried his nose deeper in his book. His mom warned him over and over again that reading in the car would make him sick, but he did it anyway. The Sherlock Holmes mystery *The Hound of the Baskervilles* was one of his favorites. Daniel had a thing for detective stories, and Sherlock Holmes was the best detective ever. Period. While Daniel was completely aware that a middle-aged, pipe-smoking British sleuth was not the typical hero of the average twelve-year-old boy, peer pressure meant little to him. He liked spending his time amidst the gaslit streets and horse-drawn carriages, the dangerous arch-criminals and, of course, trusty sidekick Dr. Watson.

Daniel sometimes wished for a trusty sidekick. All he had was Georgie, who was too young to be of much help in anything. *With a sidekick like Georgie, not even Holmes would have solved many crimes,* thought Daniel. *He would have been too busy clapping all the time.*

Besides, Daniel understood something that Georgie didn't—that his parents were clapping to get their minds off why they were moving in the first place. They were moving to Noble's Green because that was where Gram lived, and she was very, very sick. For Daniel, the best way to escape that sad fact was to disappear between the covers of a well-read book.

The moving truck was waiting for them by the time the family minivan turned onto Elm Lane, the Corrigan family's new address. The truck was backed into the driveway as far as it could reach—it was one of those big tractor-trailer types and the front cab stuck out into the street. He didn't understand why they would need all that stuff, even if they *were* going to be here for a long time. The thought of their old apartment sitting empty back in Philadelphia filled Daniel with a strange sadness.

When they pulled up, the movers were already unloading the truck.

"C'mon, Daniel," said his dad. "We'll let your mom go in and tell your gram that we're here. I'll give you the grand tour."

"Watch yourself getting out of the car, honey," said his mom as she unbuckled Georgie from his car seat. "The oncoming traffic can't see you with that big truck in the way."

His dad smiled as he gestured to the giant wraparound porch. "Pretty cool, huh?"

Gram's house was two stories tall, three if you counted the attic, and the whole thing was painted a sort of pale blue, with white doors and window frames.

"You'll get the attic bedroom—it's got a great view of the mountain—and Georgie will sleep in the one next to ours."

Daniel didn't say anything; he just focused on not looking impressed.

They ended their tour at the back of the house, next to a set of double doors. They were closed, but Daniel could hear the sound of laughter on the other side.

Daniel's father knocked very gently, and a small voice answered from the other side, "Come on in!"

His father put his hand on Daniel's shoulder and gave him a reassuring squeeze, then opened the door.

The master bedroom was bright and airy. Floor-to-ceiling

windows covered two of the walls, and the light filtered down through the trees, shining in beams along the dark wood floor. A large four-poster bed sat in the middle, and there was a soft sofa against one of the windows. Daniel's mother was holding Georgie in her lap, while a woman in a nurse's uniform perched on a stool, reading a magazine. And there, seated on the edge of the bed, was Gram. She looked thinner than he remembered and her hair seemed whiter, even though it had only been a few months since she had last visited them in Philadelphia. A small plastic hose extended from her nostrils to a tank around her waist, but she was smiling.

His father leaned down and whispered, "It's okay. Why don't you go and give your gram a hug?"

"I know. I look like something out of a movie, hooked up to all these contraptions. Robo-Gram," she said.

Daniel's initial trepidation melted away when he saw Gram wink in his direction. She might not look as strong as he remembered, but she sounded just like her old self.

He walked over and wrapped his arms around her. His gram used to smell of stale perfume and hair spray, but now she smelled of something he didn't recognize, something *mediciney*. Daniel could feel the bones of her rib cage through her shirt.

She must have read Daniel's mind. "Yeah, I'm as skinny as a bird, aren't I? It's the food they've got me on. No one around here understands the healing power of fat and grease!

But together, maybe we can convince them. What do you say to some burgers and fries?"

Daniel smiled as she patted his cheek. "You bet!" he answered. "Milk shakes?"

"Well, of course! Milk shakes go without saying."

They went on like that for a while, with Gram teasing and making Daniel laugh. It wasn't until Georgie started to get restless that Daniel's mother decided to break up the fun.

"Daniel, why don't you take your little brother outside for a bit? Let us talk for a while."

Georgie looked up hopefully at Daniel and said, "Ball." So far Georgie had been slow to talk—he only knew a few dozen words that weren't baby talk, and *ball* was definitely his favorite.

"All right," answered Daniel. "C'mon."

"Watch the traffic," called Daniel's mother as they turned and walked down the long hallway to the front door.

Daniel told Georgie to wait on the porch while he got his brother's favorite toy out of the car. Playing ball with Georgie was really quite simple—it consisted of watching Georgie drop the ball on the ground, squeal and then pick it up again. If you clapped every now and then, he was happy as could be.

When Daniel came back with the ball—a big blue-and-white-striped one—Georgie jumped up and down and started shouting, "Ball! Ball! Baaaalllllll!"

"I think he wants that ball," said a voice behind Daniel.

He turned around and found himself face to face with a

girl. She was close to his age, with straight dark hair cut short and holes in the knees of her jeans—a good sign that she was somebody who wasn't afraid to get dirty. As a rule, Daniel didn't put too much stock in girls, but this one looked as if she might be sort of okay.

"Hey," he said.

The girl didn't say anything right away. She just kind of squinted at him instead. Daniel didn't know why, but he felt suddenly self-conscious. He straightened his shoulders and ran his fingers through his tangled curls. He'd had a cap on all morning and his head looked like a matted sandy-brown mop.

Finally she spoke up. "If you don't give him that ball pretty soon, I think his head might explode."

Daniel had forgotten all about Georgie. His little brother was on his tiptoes, reaching up, trying to bat the ball out of Daniel's hands. Georgie's little face was growing bright red as he strained to grab it.

"Oh shoot!" said Daniel. "Sorry, Georgie. Here you go."

Georgie's giant frown turned to a grin as he took the big blue ball with both hands and plopped it on the ground. He laughed and made a bunch of squawky two-year-old noises as he chased the ball down the sloping yard.

"So is your family moving in with Mrs. Stewart?" asked the girl.

"Yeah, she's my gram. She's been sick, so we're here to take care of her," answered Daniel. "You live around here?"

The girl shrugged and half pointed over her shoulder. She

seemed not to care about much of anything, and that included answering Daniel's questions.

"Across the street," she said.

Again there was that uncomfortable silence. Maybe Daniel had been wrong about her. Maybe the dirty jeans were a ruse and she was just as weird as all the other girls his age. She might even have a doll hidden on her somewhere.

Well, she could stand there and stare all day long. He would just play ball with Georgie until she got tired of watching and went home to wherever it was she came from. "Across the street" somewhere, he supposed.

That was when Daniel noticed that Georgie had followed his rolling ball a little too close to the edge of the yard. If Mom saw him playing that far away from the house, she would throw a fit.

"Georgie!" Daniel called. "Come on back away from the street, okay?"

But Georgie wasn't listening. He threw the ball up in the air and laughed as it bounced off the curb and out in front of the truck. Georgie toddled after it, chasing it into the street, not paying attention to the car that was barreling toward him.

"Georgie!" Daniel screamed as he raced to his brother, knowing he would never make it in time. As Georgie disappeared into the street, Daniel heard a loud popping sound as the car came around the corner.

"GEORGIE!"

"BALL!" shouted Georgie's voice behind him.

Daniel turned to see the girl standing there, holding his little brother in her arms. Georgie was clapping. She set him down and looked past Daniel into the street.

"I think his ball just got run over," she said. "Looks like he'll need a new one."

Daniel was so relieved to see his brother safe and in one piece, he couldn't speak. But how was that possible?

"Well," she sighed, "I'd better get back. It's almost lunchtime."

Georgie gave one of his giggly little squeals, and the girl looked down at him and smiled. It was the first time Daniel had seen her do that.

"Keep a good eye on your little brother here. I think he likes trouble."

And with that she started to walk away.

"Wait!" called Daniel, breathless. His mind was racing, trying to catch up to what had just happened. He needed to stall, to have time to think. "Um, I mean . . . what's your name? I didn't get your name."

She squinted back at him again and paused before answering.

"It's Mollie," she said. "Mollie Lee. See you around, New Kid."

Then she turned and walked off toward the little yellow house directly across the street.

Chapter Two
The Bus Stop

*T*he only thing worse than your first day in a new town, thought Daniel, *is your first day in a new* school *in a new town.*

On that morning his parents offered to drive him, but Daniel knew it was hard enough being the new kid without getting chauffeured around by your parents. He knew better than to give in to the butterflies in his stomach. The first day at a new school was like the first swim in a cold lake—it was better to just dive in and get the initial shock over with. So after a quick breakfast, Daniel grabbed his brand-new backpack and walked bravely to the bus stop at the end of Elm Lane.

As he waited, he tried to distract himself by reflecting on

the mysterious Mollie Lee. It had been several days since their strange meeting, and he hadn't seen so much as a glimpse of her since then. No matter how many times he re-played the scene in his head, he could not figure out how Mollie had gotten into the street, rescued Georgie from the oncoming car, then returned to her original spot that fast—and all without Daniel seeing a thing. As something of an am-ateur sleuth, Daniel had carefully worked out three possible explanations:

The first and most likely (if least interesting) solution was that Daniel was just flat-out wrong—that when he thought he'd seen Georgie run out into the street, he had simply been mistaken. Perhaps it was just Georgie's big blue ball that rolled out there, and Daniel mistook that flash of color for his brother. The only problem with this was that Daniel had *clearly seen Georgie run out into the street*!

Which brought Daniel to the next, and somewhat more interesting, possibility—he was going insane. Perhaps he had contracted some kind of rare tropical brain fever like in the Sherlock Holmes story "The Adventure of the Dying Detective," and now he was seeing things. The upside of brain fever would be that you probably got to miss a lot of school, but the downside was, well, you had brain fever. That couldn't be all that fun. And the fact that, other than his one little hallucination, Daniel felt fine pretty much ruled out the rare disease theory.

Which left explanation number three, by far the most

exciting one: that somehow Mollie really had been quick enough to run over and save Georgie from the oncoming car and then carry him back, all before Daniel could take a single step. Either she was that fast or she made it *appear* she was that fast. Perhaps Daniel was the victim of some kind of crazy practical joke? In the Holmes stories, anything that defied explanation or seemed in some way supernatural was always a hoax.

Whatever the answer, all the evidence told him there was something very interesting about Mollie. Not the least of which was the sight of her standing right in front of him. He'd been so wrapped up in his own thoughts that he hadn't even seen her approach.

Some detective.

Mollie looked to be wearing the same pair of dirty jeans as before, though Daniel suspected that all of her jeans looked this way, since she didn't seem the type to let a good pair of jeans go undirtied. Standing next to her was a small boy about their age but a good several inches shorter. He was wearing a pair of thick glasses and a little-boy-sized tie. In stark contrast to Mollie, the way this boy was dressed reminded Daniel more of a tiny adult than a kid.

Mollie nudged the boy in the ribs. "Rohan, look, it's the new kid I told you about."

The short boy stared at Daniel, squinting at him from behind bottle-thick lenses.

Daniel waved at them.

Rohan looked back at Mollie. "Seems perfectly nice to me."

"I liked his brother better," she said.

"I thought you said his brother was, like, two?"

"Yep," she answered. "Exactly."

Daniel found this talking-about-him-as-if-he-wasn't-there thing very unsettling.

"Daniel," he said.

"Excuse me?" asked Rohan.

"Daniel. My name's Daniel. Not 'New Kid.' "

"Whatever." Mollie smirked.

"Oh," said Rohan, blinking. "Of course. Pleased to meet you, Daniel."

This Rohan kid even talked like a little adult, and sure enough, the next minute he was shaking Daniel's hand. A firm, professional handshake.

"Don't mind Mollie," said Rohan, smiling big. "She's a bit territorial, and she doesn't like it when new people show up in her neighborhood. Bears are like that, too, you know. Big, stupid bears."

Mollie just rolled her eyes and snorted, but it made Daniel relax a little to see Rohan poking fun at her without getting hit.

Rohan stopped, sniffing the air. He made a face. "Uh-oh."

"Speaking of big and stupid . . . ," said Mollie, pointing to something coming down the street.

Daniel turned to see two rough-looking boys walking toward them. Something about them just said "trouble." It was the way they walked, maybe, or the fact that they weren't carrying book bags, or books at all for that matter. They just looked tough, like the kind of boys who plan to pay for lunch with someone else's money.

"Crud," said Rohan. "It's Clay Cudgens. He and Bud must've missed the bus and decided to hike up here to our stop."

"Or they just decided to start their day off with a little 'fun,'" said Mollie. "Watch yourself around those two, New Kid."

"Yeah," echoed Rohan. "Same goes for all of us." For some reason, Rohan had put on a nose clip, the kind that you wear for swimming. Daniel had never seen a sillier sight than little Rohan standing there wearing a tie and nose clip, but he didn't have the time to comment on it, because Clay and Bud were upon them.

"Well, lookee here! It's Mollie and her girlfriend, Rohan!" shouted one of the boys. Physically he was the skinnier of the two, but something in the look of his eyes said that he was definitely the meaner. He was wearing a grotesque concert T-shirt decorated with skulls and decapitated bodies. His enormous friend's shirt was plain except for the word "Bud," which was stenciled unevenly on the front.

Daniel heard Rohan whispering to Mollie, "Just ignore them, Mol." But Mollie didn't look as if she were about to go along with Rohan's plan. Daniel could practically hear her teeth grinding together.

"Aw, yeah, Clay!" said Bud. "Rohan is Mollie's girlfriend, because Rohan is such a girl! Good one, man!" Bud's arms were a little too thick and his head was a little too small. He looked like a bald ape with a Twinkies problem.

Then there was the smell. This Bud character *stank*. At first Daniel wondered if there was some kind of roadkill nearby, or perhaps an open sewer, but before long he realized that the stink was coming off Bud. The kid had a stench that went way beyond regular body odor. It smelled like rotten garbage, if you buried it in a pile of raw fish. Then left it out in the sun. In summer. Somewhere in the Land of Stink. Rohan and Mollie were openly covering their noses. Daniel now wished he had a ridiculous-looking nose clip of his own. Even Clay seemed to have had all he could take of his friend's smell.

"Yo, Bud. Stand downwind, man. You're going to make me lose my breakfast!" said Clay.

"Sorry, dude. It gets worse when I get excited," said Bud as he stepped back a few feet from the rest of them.

"So," said Clay, sizing up Daniel. "Who's this?"

Daniel's legs turned soft and jellylike as Clay's beady eyes focused on him. It was like being looked at by a strange, mangy dog. You don't trust it, and you don't dare turn your back on it, so you just stand there—frozen.

Daniel had once read that when facing a wild animal, you should never show fear because animals can smell weakness and it only makes them hungrier. Bolstering his courage, he took a deep breath and answered, "My name's . . . uh . . . er . . . ."

Oh no! Had he just forgotten his own name?

"Uh, I'm the n-new kid," said Daniel, sounding just like lunch.

"His name's Daniel," answered Mollie, much to Daniel's surprise.

"Daaaaniel, huh?" Clay sneered as he stepped closer. He was a good several inches taller than Daniel. "So are these your new best friends, Daniel? A crazy Buddha and a girl?"

"I'm Hindu, not Buddhist," Rohan chirped.

"Shut up, no one's talking to you," said Bud from several feet away.

"So, what's the story, New Kid?" asked Clay, putting one of his long arms around Daniel's shoulders. "Are these *losers* your friends or what?"

Daniel immediately recognized what was going on—Clay was giving him a choice. In Clay's eyes, Daniel was a blank slate, a new kid with no allegiances. He could become friends with anyone—with Rohan, Mollie, a couple of bullies like Clay and Bud. Trouble was, in order to befriend a bully, you had to become one.

Daniel was going to have to go with the short kid and the tomboy.

"Yeah," he said, gesturing to Mollie and Rohan. "I guess they are my friends."

Clay's eyes narrowed to tiny slits. "Too bad for you, New

Kid," he said. "Just for that, I think I'll take that nice new backpack you're wearing. I left mine at home."

Clay gave Daniel's backpack a little tug. Daniel held firm. He knew he wasn't a match for these two, but that didn't mean he was going to give in this easy.

"C'mon, *New Kid,*" said Bud, leering. "You don't want to get hurt, do you?"

Still, Daniel wouldn't let go. He wasn't a fighter, but if he gave up now, these two would hound him for the rest of the year. Daniel had no intention of being marked as an easy target.

An ugly look crept over Clay's face. "Warned you."

Clay pulled again, only this time much harder. Impossibly hard. Daniel felt his feet leave the ground, and when his head finally stopped spinning, he realized that Clay had thrown him twelve feet at least. This boy was stronger than a grown man—stronger than *ten* grown men.

Mollie came to his rescue. Daniel didn't even see her move but there she was, standing face to face with Clay, yelling at him to return Daniel's backpack. Bud began giggling like a hyena and the air grew thick with his stench.

Daniel was bruised up a bit, and his head was still ringing from being thrown around like a rag doll, but he wasn't about to sit by and let Mollie fight this fight for him, no matter how strong Clay might be.

"I can handle this," said Daniel, getting to his feet. "Give me back my bag, Clay."

"Oh, the new kid's a scrapper, huh?" said Clay, looking over Mollie's head. "Okay, tell you what—if you can take this backpack from me, you can have it. I'll even let you have the first punch. Bud, grab me one of those rocks."

Bud reached down and picked up a fist-sized rock from the side of the road. Daniel swallowed hard. A rock like that could seriously hurt someone, or worse.

"Give it to him," said Clay.

Bud tossed the rock to Daniel, who caught it awkwardly with both hands.

What was this kid up to? Was he crazy?

"Okay, give me your best shot."

Daniel hesitated, staring at the heavy rock in his hand.

"C'mon, Daniel. I've even given you a weapon! Hit me as hard as you can."

Daniel felt sick to his stomach as Clay smiled a wicked smile.

"Of course, then it'll be my turn," said Clay. "But I promise I'll only use my fist."

This was turning very serious.

"That's enough, Clay!" shouted Mollie.

"This is none of your business, Mollie," answered Clay evenly. "It's between me and Daniel here."

"I'm making it my business," said Mollie through clenched teeth. "He lives on my block, so I'm gonna look out for him. Give him his backpack. Now!"

Clay paused. There was a flash of something almost like

worry across his face, and Bud was no longer laughing. Then Clay spat on the ground in front of Mollie.

"Fine! You want to get into it, too? I've been waiting for this day for a long time. Let's see just how fast you are, little girl!" Clay took a step forward and balled his hands into fists. Mollie stood firm, but Daniel could see the fear in her eyes. There had to be some way to stop this.

It was Rohan who broke it up. He stepped between the two of them and tapped Clay on the arm. Rohan calmly looked up at the towering Clay and said, "Clay? If you hurt Mollie, Eric will hear about it, you know he will. Are you prepared to 'get into it' with him, too?"

Clay glared down at Rohan, his face red with anger and the veins in his temple ready to burst. He looked as if he wanted nothing more than to smash everything in sight, but he didn't. Instead, he put his fists down, tossed Daniel his backpack and cursed under his breath.

"Have it your way," he said. "But no one stays a kid forever—not even Eric. I *promise* you, very soon things in this town are gonna change. Then you'll all get what's coming to you. You too, *New Kid*. Congrats, you just made my Enemies List."

With that, Clay stalked off down the road. Bud looked around anxiously and called, "But, Clay, we'll miss the bus again! It's the last stop and we'll miss school! Dude, my mom will kill me!"

Clay kept walking, saying nothing. Bud stood there for a few more seconds before chasing after him, taking the cloud of foulness with him.

Mollie and Rohan watched them go in silence. Daniel wanted to shout or laugh or something, but the other two seemed so deep in thought, so full of worry, that he didn't say anything. He just waited for the bus with his new friends, a million questions swirling around in his head.

Chapter Three
The Bridge

There was definitely something a little strange about the kids of Noble's Green.

Daniel had seen girls stand up to bullies before, but that was usually because they were armed with the knowledge that the bully wouldn't hit a girl. But Clay had been ready to fight Mollie, girl or no, and she'd looked ready for it. She had been willing to stick up for Daniel, someone she barely knew, even if it meant tussling with someone as strong as Clay Cudgens.

Sitting in his new homeroom class on this, his first day at school, Daniel wished he were half as bold as Mollie Lee. He felt the stares of his new classmates, and all the attention was making him wish he could just disappear beneath his desk. Daniel had never considered himself a brave person to begin with, and he'd used up what little reserve of courage he had with Clay that morning. He was in full coward mode now.

"Hey, Daniel."

He turned in his seat and saw Rohan sitting down at the desk next to him. To see a familiar face, even one he'd only met an hour ago, was an immeasurable relief.

"Listen, at recess do you want me to show you around? Keep you from wandering into the elementary schoolers' yard, stuff like that? I feel bad about what happened earlier, and I'd like to prove that this place isn't always like that."

"Okay. Thanks, I guess."

"You see, Noble's Green is a really small town, and great as it is, it's more of a place that people move away *from,* not *to.* Understand?"

"Kind of."

Rohan's face broke out in a silly grin. "You know, you're almost a celebrity!"

"A lot of good it did me so far. I wouldn't call getting knocked on your butt the celebrity treatment."

A couple of girls a few seats over looked Daniel's way and started to giggle. Suddenly he longed to be back at the bus stop facing Clay and Bud—getting beaten up he could handle, but the whole girl thing, it was just too gruesome.

"Hey," Daniel said quietly, interrupting Rohan's speech

on the shortest route to the bathroom. "Tell me something—just how strong *is* Clay?"

Rohan shifted in his seat, clearly uncomfortable. "Well, he's pretty strong."

"Yeah, I was on the receiving end of that. He's what? Twelve? Thirteen? . . ."

"He just turned twelve," said Rohan quickly.

"Okay," said Daniel. "My point is, he tossed me straight up into the air! A grown man couldn't throw me like that."

Rohan shook his head. "No, no. You must've hit your head or something. From what I saw, he . . . he only shoved you a little. Your feet never left the ground."

He was lying, and doing it badly. What's more, the whole conversation was obviously making him very uncomfortable. He kept stealing glances over his shoulder and had lowered his voice. Daniel was on to something. His detective sense was tingling.

"Look, I didn't imagine it! He tossed me around like a sack of pota—"

"It's impossible, Daniel! It's like you said, no one's *that* strong! No one!"

"Rohan Parmar, do you have something you'd like to share with the rest of the class? Considering that it is nine o'clock, class has started and you are, for some reason, still talking?"

Mr. Snyder, Daniel's new homeroom teacher, had appeared at the front of the class. Daniel had taken an immediate dislike to him. Although he'd been perfectly nice to Daniel when they'd met earlier, there was something in the way he looked at you that just seemed . . . mean. He held his nose a little too high in the air and squinted a little too hard.

"Uh, no, sir, Mr. Snyder. I was just telling Daniel here how to get around."

"Well, while I'm sure that Daniel appreciates your hospitality, please save the tour-guide act for after class."

"Yessir."

"Well, now that I have the floor in my own class, I would like to welcome our newest student, Mr. Daniel Corrigan. Daniel has come all the way from Philadelphia to our little town. I trust that you all will make him feel welcome. Now, if you would please open your textbooks. We are going to begin with a little review of statistical graphs. . . ."

As Daniel cracked open his book, he was relieved to see that the rest of the class had apparently already grown bored with him and were now focused, painfully, on the lesson at hand. All except for Mollie Lee. He spied her near the front of the class, giving him a sideways stare, her face unreadable.

Daniel sank even lower in his seat, his chin nearly level with the top of the desk. Any lower and he'd melt into the floor.

At that moment the classroom door flew open and . . . *something* came through. It was roughly boy-shaped, but this thing was soaking wet and covered in filth. Its clothes were streaked with mud and it smelled like the bottom of a lake.

And it was smiling a big, bright smile.

For a moment, no one said anything.

"Eric Johnson!" Mr. Snyder said, finally. "What . . . how dare . . . for goodness' sake, boy, you are soaking wet!"

The boy wrung a bit of greenish water from his shirt. "Yeah, about that . . . I had a little spill on the way here. But I made it on time, didn't I?"

The class broke out into a fit of giggles. Everyone, Daniel noticed, except Mollie and Rohan. They saw what was coming.

Mr. Snyder's face turned purple with rage. "In fact, Mr. Johnson, you are late! And you will NOT be let into my class looking like that!"

"I'm really sorry, Mr. Snyder. I'll go and change into my gym clothes."

"And then you will go to the principal's office. You will not come back here."

"But, Mr. Snyder, I tried to get here on time, I really did."

"And again, you failed. I'd call your mother and have her come and pick you up, but that would be a waste of time, wouldn't it?"

When Eric answered, it was little more than a whisper. Any hint of a smile was gone, and his mouth hardened into a solid line.

"My mom's at work."

"Of course she is." Now Mr. Snyder smiled, but there wasn't any warmth in it. In that one grin, he confirmed all of Daniel's earlier misgivings about him. Mr. Snyder was just another bully.

"Now off to the principal's office with you. I don't want to hear another word."

Eric turned and headed for the door. Then Daniel saw him mouth something to Mollie. It looked as if he were saying "tangled leak." Daniel wished he were better at reading lips.

"Now, where were we?" said Mr. Snyder, smiling once again. "Ah, yes, statistical graphs . . ."

The next morning Daniel played with his cereal as pieces of a puzzle whirled around in his brain. But he couldn't fit them anywhere. He looked up only when his father let out one of his low whistles that usually meant "that was a doozy." His parents were discussing something in the paper.

"It's darn lucky no one was seriously hurt," Gram was saying.

"It really is a miracle," said his mother.

"Not quite a miracle," said Daniel's father, looking at the paper. "Says here that the police suspect that the couple was actually rescued by a passerby. The driver of the car had vague memories of being pulled out of the car and lifted from the bottom of the river! Can you believe that?"

Gram shook her head. "They should've condemned that thing years ago. I've always said that the Tangle Creek Bridge is nothing but a death trap. . . ."

Gram kept talking but Daniel was no longer listening. He was picturing Eric standing there in his dripping clothes and smiling that big, *proud* smile. A piece of the puzzle popped into place.

Tangle Creek Bridge.

Chapter Four

The Incident at the Observatory

For the next several days Daniel watched Rohan, Eric and Mollie very closely. In turn, they watched him. On the day after the bridge accident, Daniel followed Mollie home from school, only to turn around and find Rohan following him. Daniel had been standing across the street from Mollie's house, waiting for her to . . . well, he didn't know exactly, but he was sure she was up to something strange . . . when he'd heard a sneeze behind him. Sure enough, there was Rohan, looking miserable in a patch of pollen-dusted wildflowers. When pressed, Rohan claimed that his dog, Shaggy, had run off, but Daniel knew better. Daniel had seen Shaggy and he was by far the oldest dog he'd ever met. Shaggy wouldn't be running anywhere.

Rohan was a bizarre kid, no doubt, yet despite everything the two were fast becoming friends. But Rohan's behavior was definitely strange. Sometimes he would put on his nose clip or even stuff earplugs in his ears for no reason whatsoever. And Rohan had a tendency to zone out. He'd be in the middle of a heated defense of pirating over detective work and suddenly start staring off into space. Daniel had to practically shake him to get him to come back to earth.

Mollie hung out with them occasionally, but she barely paid any attention to Daniel. Sometimes she would talk with Rohan about school or sports, but most of her time she spent with Eric.

Eric. After the story of the rescue at the Tangle Creek Bridge, Daniel had decided that if there was a mystery to be solved here, the answer lay with Eric. He seemed nice enough—always smiling, always easygoing—but for some reason Daniel had been unable to work up the courage to talk to him. Daniel had noticed that Eric missed a lot of school, and he suspected that it wasn't because of illness. Whatever the case, both Mollie and Rohan were fiercely protective of him. Whenever Daniel started to ask questions, they would quickly change the subject. If he pressed on, they would eventually get mad and just walk away. Daniel had the feeling that if forced to choose between their secrets and him, they'd choose their secrets.

All of which put Daniel into a rather foul mood during those next few weeks. His gloom and the increasingly secretive behavior of his new "friends" meant that when the first field trip of the year came around, he was ready for it. The visit to the Mount Noble Observatory was the *one* thing he'd been looking forward to since coming to Noble's Green. The observatory belonged to the university and had one of the most powerful telescopes in the country, as well as a planetarium complete with a laser-light star show. But best of all, the trip was a chance for Daniel to think about something other than his new stack of problems.

When they arrived at the observatory, the students were given a half hour to tour the museum displays and gift shop. Like the rest of his classmates, Daniel was itching to blow his allowance on some souvenir junk, and was on his way to do just that when he saw Clay and Bud waiting for him outside the gift shop. As Bud looked his way, Daniel beat a quick retreat up a nearby staircase to avoid a potential pounding.

When he reached the top, he found his way blocked. A large sign read "No Admittance—Exhibit Closed for Repairs," and the hall was roped off with yellow caution tape. But he didn't want to face Clay and Bud, and since there was no other way around, he slipped under the tape and went inside.

The hall looked empty except for some sheets of drywall and a few power tools littering the floor. The room smelled of sawdust and fresh paint—just the sort of place that would play havoc with Rohan's allergies. Although the electricity was off, the room was bright with daylight. It poured in through a giant hole in the outside wall, where the floor ended in a sheer drop. Peeking over the side, Daniel could see that they had started to erect scaffolding several floors below. Beyond that was nothing but empty air. It was a long way down the mountain from up here.

In one corner of the hall, there was a large sheet of plastic, billowing in the wind. Behind it, Daniel found an intact exhibit, complete with dioramas and photographs, detailing the history of Mount Noble and the building of the observatory. Some of the photographs dated back to the beginning of the twentieth century, when Noble's Green was just a burgeoning trade town. In one photograph, brown and blurry with age, a ragtag group of children stood with a bearded man dressed in skins and a fur cap. The caption read "Jonathan Noble and the survivors of the St. Alban's fire. This photograph was taken after the survivors emerged from the wilderness of Mount Noble."

There was more written there, something about the burning of an orphanage and how its children were all saved by a local trapper named Jonathan Noble. Daniel was just beginning to read about the suspected cause of the fire when he caught the whiff of something bad. Something nauseatingly familiar.

"Well, if it isn't Daaaaniel, all by his lonesome."

Daniel recognized the voice. It had the gravelly pitch of someone used to shouting.

Clay was standing there in the doorway of the little history exhibit, blocking Daniel's exit. His arms were folded in front of him, and he was wearing an ugly smile. Bud was off to the side, writing "BUD RULES" in black marker across one of the walls.

This was a bad situation. Here Daniel was, in a place that was off-limits, with no teachers around, trapped with the two most dangerous kids in school. He didn't even have Mollie to stick up for him now. This time he was on his own. He remembered Clay's "Enemies List" and the thought made him queasy.

"Where's your girlfriend?" asked Clay, looking around.

Something occurred to Daniel then, giving him a tiny bit of hope that he hadn't had before—Clay was scared of something. He was being cautious, hesitant even. Maybe Rohan's threat about Eric still had a hold on the little thug, and if Daniel used it to his advantage, he just might make it out of here in one piece.

"She's around," Daniel croaked. He hadn't realized it until now, but his mouth had gone dry. He wondered if they could see his legs shaking. Would they be satisfied that they had simply terrified him and leave it at that? Somehow Daniel doubted it.

"In fact, Mollie and Eric are on their way up here right now, so you'd better get out of my way."

Then he did something either very brave or very crazy— he started walking straight toward them, as if they weren't even there. The way he figured it, he had one chance—Clay and Bud were both bigger than him, and Clay was certainly way stronger, but they weren't the brightest couple of kids.

He needed to bluff them, and quick, before they recognized the lie on his face.

Amazingly, it worked. Or at least it started to. Bud knitted his brow, clearly thrown by Daniel's brazen approach, and backed up a step to the right, giving Daniel just enough room to squeeze by. Clay, however, stood perfectly still, watching Daniel pass. He looked as if he were thinking so hard it hurt.

Daniel was maybe three steps past them when he heard Clay sneer, "Aw, this is bull! He's up here all alone!"

That's when Daniel ran. He sprinted as fast as he could on wobbly legs toward the stairs, not even daring to look back at the sound of footsteps pursuing him. He could feel someone's hot breath on the back of his neck and tripped just as fingers grabbed at his shirt collar.

Daniel skidded on his hands and knees and ended up in a pile on the floor, dangerously close to the exposed wall and the sheer drop down the mountainside. The bright sunlight was streaming in from outside, and Daniel shielded his eyes from the glare. He was dazed from his fall and blinded by the sun, but he could still hear Clay's mocking laughter somewhere in front of him. He was trapped between Clay and the deadly fall. The air around him smelled strongly of rotting stink, of dead things.

"Nowhere to go, New Kid. Might as well take what's coming to you."

In a panic, Daniel got to his feet too fast and realized the room was spinning. He'd fallen harder than he'd thought, and now his vision began to go dark with spots. Stumbling and blind, he tried to back away from Clay's taunting laughter.

Daniel's eyes started to clear just in time to see Clay make a desperate grab for him. Daniel lunged backward. But the look on Clay's face suddenly changed. The cruel smile disappeared and his eyes went wide with fear. He shouted, "Wait! Look out!" but it was too late. Daniel was already taking another step back, but this time he found only empty air. Daniel's stomach dropped out from under him as he tottered over and through the exposed wall, plummeting off the side of Mount Noble.

All Daniel saw was the blurry shape of the scaffolding passing by him, and all he heard was the sound of blood pounding in his ears. Despite his panic, he found himself wondering whether he would feel it when he hit, or if he would just die instantly.

Then he was no longer falling. Somebody had a hold of him, and that someone was floating in midair.

He turned his head and saw Eric smiling back at him.

"Hi, Daniel. I guess it's time we talked, huh?"

Chapter Five
The Children of Noble's Green

"So, I guess I'd better start with introductions. Well, that's Louisa and her little sister, Rose. Louisa can walk through stuff and Rose can turn invisible. That's Simon—he can do things with electricity. It's pretty cool, you'll see. You already know Rohan—nothing gets past him. He can see and hear and smell just about anything. And, of course, Mollie—the best flier there ever was—"

"Not ever," interrupted Mollie. "Michael was better."

The room went silent as Eric glared at Mollie, but she just returned his stare.

"All right," continued Eric. "Mollie here is the *fastest* flier there ever was. And unfortunately, you've already met Clay and Bud—we don't hang out with them."

Eric smiled at the last bit, and Daniel's own mouth, he knew, was still hanging wide open. He was standing in an old tree fort deep in the woods of Mount Noble—the kids' secret hideout. With two rooms and a tire swing, it was massive by tree-fort standards, and the supporting branches of two great oaks practically sagged under the weight. Newly painted boards covered up patches of rot here and there, but overall this place had been kept in excellent shape despite its obvious age and use. Freshly tied rope ladders dangled from the sides, and there was even a pirate crow's nest made from discarded roof shingles.

The walls inside were covered with posters and hand-drawn pictures. Some of them were just typical kids' stuff like rockets or race cars, even a few baby animals. But most were drawings of children. In crayon, finger paint or Magic Marker, there were pictures of children laughing, children flying, even children lifting cars over their heads. But as intriguing as the actual pictures were, what shocked Daniel the most was just how old some of them looked—drawn on yellowing paper, with images so faded as to be nearly unrecognizable. Someone had been drawing these for many, many years.

"That's all of us, Daniel," Eric finished. "The Supers of Noble's Green."

"Man, I hate it when he says things like that," said Simon,

a plump boy with spiky blond hair. He mumbled it under his breath, but still loud enough for everyone to hear. But Eric just ignored him and turned to Daniel.

"So," he said. "What do you think?"

What Daniel wanted to say right then was "I think you've all gone super-insane and I'm right there with you." But he didn't. He thought he should at least *try* being polite to the boy who had, earlier that day, saved his life. . . .

After saving Daniel from the terrible fall, Eric had carried him—no, *flown* him—around the side of the observatory to a safe landing spot.

Mollie was there to greet them. She looked worried, but Daniel wondered whether she was concerned about his safety or about the fact that he now knew Eric's secret. His head was spinning from the shock of it all.

Eric saw the look on his face. "Listen, Daniel, I know you're pretty freaked out right now, but I need you to stay cool for a while, okay? I promise I'll tell you everything you want to know later, but right now we need to act like nothing happened. All right? Daniel?"

Daniel's heart still felt as if it were going to burst from his chest, but despite it all he almost laughed in Eric's face. What choice did Eric think he had? Should he go tell a teacher that a super-bully and his smelly sidekick had chased him out a hole on top of the observatory, but since a flying super-kid caught him, now everything was okay?

Mollie stepped forward and put her hand on Daniel's

shoulder. "Please, Daniel. I promise we'll tell you everything, just a little later."

And with that touch, Daniel's heart stopped racing and he was able to catch his breath and calm down. He was still in shock, but Mollie's hand was reassuring.

"Yeah," he said, nodding. "Okay. We'll talk later."

Eric smiled. "Great, Daniel. Be at your bedroom window tonight around nine o'clock. We'll meet you there." Eric paused while he and Mollie exchanged looks. "And thanks, Daniel. For trusting us."

Eric and Daniel returned to the observatory and snuck into the planetarium, where the rest of the class was already watching the star show. Eric leaned back in his chair and grinned at the many colored lights overhead, but for Daniel, it all went by in a blur.

When they got back to the bus, Rohan was waiting for them. He looked genuinely relieved to see Daniel alive and well.

"Man, oh man," he was saying. "Are you all right?"

Daniel nodded and then climbed aboard the bus, silent.

Behind him, Rohan was still muttering, "Man, oh man."

Just as the bus was about to pull away, Clay and Bud dragged themselves on board. Bud stared at his shoes as he walked and the air around him was strangely odor-free, but Clay held his head high, defiant. When they walked by Daniel's seat, Clay leaned down and whispered, "What were you thinkin' backing out of that window? You some kinda maniac? You almost got us in a whole mess of trouble!"

Daniel was dumbfounded. Was Clay actually blaming him for falling out of the window?

Daniel muddled through the rest of the day in a near state of shock. At 9:05 p.m., he saw Eric and Mollie standing outside in his yard, in the shadow of his house. He cautiously waved down to them and Mollie called back, "Ready?"

But they didn't wait for his answer. They just lifted off the ground and floated up to Daniel's window. Eric reached out an arm to Daniel. "Want to take a trip?"

Daniel hesitated and Eric said, "You'll be perfectly safe. Trust me."

It was like one of those trust exercises where you fall back into your friends' arms, hoping they will be there to catch you. Only Daniel was stepping out of a third-story window and Eric was not his friend. Not yet anyway.

In the end he just closed his eyes and jumped.

Eric put Daniel on his back and told him to hang on tight, and then the three of them were off—flying over the trees and houses, soaring through the dark. Mollie shouted above the rushing wind, "See you there," and sped off ahead of them.

"Show-off," Eric said as he and Daniel followed a good distance behind her, drifting through the night sky over Noble's Green, toward the dark woods of the mountainside.

Now Daniel was sitting in the secret tree fort of a bunch of super-kids.

"So, Daniel," said Eric. "What do you think?"

Daniel looked around at the kids' expectant faces. "Are you joking?"

Eric laughed. He was the type who laughed easily and often, and Daniel was finding it almost impossible not to smile along with him. But until he found some answers, he was determined to try.

"So you all have . . ." Daniel tried to think of a word that wouldn't sound as ridiculous as the one that popped into his head, but he couldn't. "So you all have . . . *superpowers?*"

"Wow, what gave it away? Maybe it was the *flying boy* who brought you here!" said the kid with the spiky hair, Simon. Turning to Eric, he let out a loud chuckle. "You sure you didn't drop this one on his head?"

"Save it, Simon," said Eric. "Yes, Daniel. We all have superpowers."

Rohan said, "Well, I like to think of them as extra-normal abilities. . . ."

"And Rohan's power is that he's a super-nerd!" offered Simon.

"Simon!" shouted Mollie and Eric at the same time.

Daniel shook his head and rubbed his eyes with the palms of his hands. This was all way too much to take in. Here he was somewhere in the wilds of Mount Noble talking to a bunch of super-kids in their . . . Tree House of Justice, or whatever. This could have been any ordinary group of kids huddled around their flashlights on a sleepover, but for the fact that there was *nothing* ordinary about these kids. Of that, at least, Daniel was sure.

"How? I mean, this is all impossible, right?"

"Rohan?" said Eric. "Would you do the honors?"

"Sure thing," said Rohan, standing. Eric gave Rohan the floor and sat down in his spot. "Well, Daniel," Rohan continued, "the truth is that we don't really know how we got these abilities, but we do know that there have been kids like us in Noble's Green for a very, very long time."

"Kids only?" asked Daniel. "You mean there aren't any adults . . . like you? Your parents aren't . . ."

"Heck no. All the adults here are as normal as you are. My parents would ground me until college if they found out."

"Go ahead," said Mollie. "Tell him. Tell him what happens."

"I'm getting there, Mol. First things first!"

"See, Daniel," Rohan went on, "for a long time Noble's Green has been a special place. For years, certain children here have been displaying these special abilities. Some of us think it goes back hundreds of years or more, but no one's really sure. What we do know is that each generation of special children passes down the four rules to the next."

"What rules?"

Rohan pointed his flashlight at Eric, who took over. "First Rule: Use Your Powers to Help. Never Hurt."

Next Rohan turned the spotlight on Louisa, who said softly, "Second Rule: The North Face and the Old Quarry Are Off-Limits. Danger Waits for Us There."

Then came Mollie. She seemed reluctant at first, but Eric gave her a little nudge in the ribs and she stood up. "Third Rule: It Ends at Thirteen."

Finally Rohan turned the light back on himself. "And most important, the Fourth Rule: Never, Ever Let Grown-ups Know."

"Not even Clay will break that one," said Eric.

"So, wait a minute," said Daniel. "You all were born with superpowers and a bunch of rules to go with them? Like an instruction manual? *The Supers' How-To Book?*"

"We weren't born with them," answered Eric, patiently ignoring Daniel's sarcasm. "They show up in us at different times. Rose here is the youngest that I know of. . . ."

"I'm five and a half!" she shouted, smiling big. "And Eric tells me the rules so I can tell them to other super-kids some-day. And Michael told them to him and . . . *somebody* told them to Michael." Rose looked a lot like her older sister, Louisa—dark skin, pretty black hair worn long and a friendly face. Unlike Mollie, when the two sisters saw Daniel staring, they answered him with welcoming smiles.

"The point is that these rules have been around forever," continued Eric. "Like the drawings and this fort, kids have been passing them on to each other for years and years. Everyone follows the rules."

"Not everyone," said Mollie.

"Well, yeah. There is the occasional bad apple."

Daniel knew right away who they were talking about. The memory of Clay chasing him off the top of the observatory was still painfully fresh.

"Tell him the rest," said Mollie. "Tell him about the Third Rule."

Rohan gave Mollie a tired look. "All right, Mol, all right. See, Daniel, the reason there are no adults like us is because of the Third Rule: It Ends at Thirteen. No one keeps their powers past their thirteenth birthday."

"You mean you give up your powers?" asked Daniel. "Just like that?"

"No, not exactly. We don't just give them up. . . . The truth is, we don't know what really happens. We don't know how we got these powers, and we also don't know how we lose them. But when I wake up on my thirteenth birthday, I will be just like you, and with no memory of ever even having powers. It all just disappears."

"Just like that," Simon said. "You go to sleep special and you wake up just a regular dweeb like everyone else."

This time Eric kicked Simon right in the shin. "Ow!" he yelped. "What did you do that for . . . oh."

Daniel's face was red, he could feel it. Everyone was looking at him. The "regular dweeb" was blushing.

"Yeah, whatever. Sorry," said Simon.

"Never mind, it's no sweat," answered Daniel, but what else could he say? It was true. Here he was, just an ordinary kid standing in a room full of superheroes. He felt very small. Very small indeed.

But that feeling didn't squelch Daniel's natural curiosity. A secret group of super-children? A set of mysterious rules passed on from kid to kid? None of this made any sense.

"So where did these rules come from, then? I mean, who wrote them?"

"Tell him! 'Bout Johnny!" said a voice in Daniel's ear, but when he turned to ask who this Johnny person was, no one was there. "Johnny! Tell him!" repeated the empty air.

"Rose! You know better than to talk to someone when they can't see you. It's not polite," said Louisa. She came over and sat next to Daniel, but she wasn't looking at him. She was looking at the empty space immediately next to him.

Rose appeared only inches away from Daniel's face. "Sorry."

"Who's Johnny?" asked Daniel, trying not to appear startled by Rose's sudden-appearing act.

Louisa answered for her sister. "Johnny Noble. He was the first of us, and he was the writer of the Rules—we think. He was a real, true superhero."

"It's only a legend," said Mollie.

"Well, actually there is some evidence," Rohan put in.

Daniel interrupted them. The kids here had a habit of talking to him as if he had some idea of what was going on. It was getting irritating. "Jonathan Noble? You mean the guy the town is named after?"

"He was more than that," said Eric. "Much more."

Daniel heard some rustling behind him and turned to see Rose digging around in an old trunk in the corner. She returned with a large stack of what looked like comic books, which she very carefully placed in front of him. Even though they were wrapped in plastic, Daniel could still smell the age on them.

Despite Louisa's flashlight, Daniel had trouble making out the details in the dark.

"We need some more light," Eric said. "Simon?"

With a grin, Simon began furiously rubbing his palms together as Daniel felt the hair on the back of his neck stand up. The room began to smell like the air before a thunderstorm.

Electricity, remembered Daniel.

There was a tiny flutter of light, then another, and another. Within a few minutes, the tree house was lit by twenty or so little glowing spheres of energy, each one no bigger than a golf ball. They crackled and popped as they floated above the children's heads.

"Whoa," said Daniel.

"They're my wisps," said Simon, smiling proudly.

"But don't touch them," warned Louisa. "Or you'll get yourself a little shock."

"Stingers," said Rose.

"You buncha babies," said Simon, but Daniel noticed that he wasn't touching them, either.

By the light of Simon's wisps, Daniel saw that the comic books were indeed old—yellowed and faded with age. Little Rose leaned over Daniel's shoulder and pointed.

"Johnny Noble," she whispered.

Across the top of every book, printed in big, bold lettering, was the title—FANTASTIC FUTURES, STARRING

Johnny Noble. The hero of every cover was a masked man in a skintight red shirt and black pants. In each drawing he was doing some different heroic deed, but most of them involved fighting Nazi tanks or punching out Axis soldiers. All these comics were obviously from the World War II era but were in relatively good shape considering their years. They were probably worth a small fortune.

Daniel was confused. These were comic books about a superhero, a character named Johnny Noble, but *Jonathan Noble* was a real man, flesh and blood. He was a local hero, sure, and while Daniel assumed there were a few tall tales about him, like the one about George Washington chopping down the cherry tree, he was definitely a real man. Daniel remembered the photo he saw hanging in the observatory. But the character in these comics was shown doing impossible things like lifting three-ton tanks and flying.

Yeah, impossible things like flying.

"You're trying to tell me that this is the same guy? That Jonathan Noble, the hero of Noble's Green, is—"

"Also known as Johnny Noble, a superhero from World War II." Eric sat down next to Daniel and took one of the books from him. Very gently, he removed it from its protective wrapper and opened it, careful not to put too much pressure on the pages. On the cover was an illustration of Johnny Noble in a dark forest, jumping from foxhole to foxhole and tearing up machine-gun nests and enemy barbed wire.

"Eric!" said Daniel. "Those are comic books, not history books!" Daniel found himself pacing around the room. His earlier shock had worn off and his logical detective mind was taking over.

Eric just shook his head. "There's more, Daniel. Among the Supers there has always been a legend of a boy who grew up *and* kept his powers. The story goes that one of the first of us was so strong and so heroic that he reached thirteen and he kept his powers. See, it's like a test—we were given these powers, and we have to prove that we are responsible enough to keep them. We have to prove that we *are* heroes."

"And why do you think that this boy, the one who grew up, is Johnny Noble?"

Rohan took the book from Eric. "Well, obviously no one knows for sure. But it's a theory."

Rohan was interrupted by a choking, gasping sound, and Daniel turned to see Simon sticking a finger down his throat.

"Oh, don't mind me," said Simon. "I'm just going to make myself *vomit* if these two don't shut up soon."

Eric folded his arms across his chest and sighed. Simon looked pleased with himself.

"Okay," said Daniel, rubbing his eyes. "Answer this—if there really was some kind of superhero fighting on our side during World War II—some Super who grew up and decided to fight crime and the whole thing—why haven't we heard about it? You'd think it might have been mentioned some-place other than a bunch of comics."

Eric shrugged. "Why haven't we heard the truth about aliens and UFOs? And ghosts and Bigfoot and stuff? It's the government! It's all over the television how the government is keeping things like that a secret. Well, what if they decided they wanted to keep him a secret, too? But someone here knew about him and published his stories in a way that guaranteed that the kids of Noble's Green would read about him—comics! The government probably erased all evidence of Johnny Noble's existence when he refused to keep working for them after the war . . . or something like that." Eric set down the copy of *Fantastic Futures* very gently, almost reverently. "Now all we have are these few."

Of everything Daniel had heard here in this tree-fort-turned-secret-hideout, this was perhaps the hardest to swallow. It must be a terrible thing to be special and have no idea why. Gram was fond of saying that everyone was looking for their purpose in life but only a few found it. These were probably the most special children on the face of the planet, and they were clinging to a bunch of old comics and conspiracy theories for answers.

In Noble's Green, kids might fly, but comic books were still just comic books.

But Daniel was too exhausted and far too overwhelmed to keep talking. Let Eric and Rose and all the rest hold on to the hope that maybe, just maybe, they might make it past their thirteenth birthday with their powers intact and grow up to be a real superhero like Johnny Noble. What was the harm in dreaming?

Daniel was tired—tired of asking questions and tired of

believing in the unbelievable. But he still had one last question that needed answering, and it was perhaps the most important one of all.

"Why me?"

"What do you mean?" asked Eric.

"Why tell me all this? I'm not like you; I can't do any of the things you do. So why share all this with me? You didn't have to save me—you could have let me fall and your secret would have been safe!"

Eric stood up and looked Daniel in the eye. He was no longer smiling.

"It's the First Rule," he said. "And it's one that I take very seriously—Use Your Powers to Help. Never Hurt. I think your death would've hurt a lot of people, Daniel."

"Me, for starters," said Rohan. "We're friends, Daniel. Aren't we?" Daniel glanced around at the room full of smiling faces. He was very uncomfortable again and could feel himself squirming under all that attention.

"I know it's been hard these last few days," continued Rohan. "And that you had questions I couldn't answer. But the truth is, we just weren't sure what to do about you. We knew you were catching on, but we don't have any friends that are . . . well, not like us. Then when Eric saw you in trouble, there was really no decision left to make."

"So now it's up to you, Daniel," said Eric. "You know all about us, and what you do with that information is your call. We can't stop you if you decide to tell."

Daniel was just about to disagree with Eric—with all

their powers, Daniel figured they could pretty much do whatever they wanted—when Rose appeared again at his side. "Never Hurt," she whispered.

Daniel looked at them all. Rohan was smiling; Eric was grinning, too. The others looked anxious, even a little afraid. Even the loudmouth, Simon. Only Mollie was hard to read. She wasn't smiling, but she wasn't wearing her usual scowl, either. She was just watching, curious as a cat.

"Yeah, I guess your secret's safe with me," answered Daniel. What else could he say?

"Great!" shouted Eric, slapping him on the back. Daniel could feel the power behind it. "I knew Rohan was right, I knew we could trust you, Daniel Corrigan!"

"Yeah, great. Go, team," said Daniel. "But it's getting a little late. Do you think we could call it a night and I could maybe, I dunno, get a ride home?"

"Sure," Eric laughed. "Glad to. I'll be your limo and chauffeur all in one."

Eric opened the tree-fort door and they stepped out onto a narrow wooden porch. From their vantage point they could see down the side of the mountain and up into the night sky—it was a bright blanket of stars.

Eric put his hand (gently this time) on Daniel's shoulder and gave it a little squeeze. "Only this time you should try keeping your eyes open, because there's really nothing like it, Daniel. Nothing at all."

Chapter Six
Flight

Eric was right. When Daniel forced himself to relax and let go of his fear, it was the single greatest experience of his life.

He was flying.

Well, technically Eric was the one doing the flying—Daniel was just along for the ride. But what a ride it was. They stayed fairly low: only twenty or thirty feet above the treetops (Eric said if they went much higher, it would get too cold for Daniel). But down here Daniel could relish the feeling of the warm air blowing his hair, and every now and then Eric would find an air current to ride and dive sharply through the mist only to rise slowly again into the night. As they glided through the dark, Daniel allowed himself a little pretending, and he imagined that he was alone. That *he* was the boy who could fly, that he was just as special as the rest of them.

"Never thought you'd see Noble's Green like this, huh, Daniel?" asked Eric, startling him from his daydream. "I know it seems like a boring little town, but once you've seen it from way up here . . . well, I wouldn't live anywhere else."

Daniel had to agree. At night, from above, it looked like a sea of twinkling stars surrounded by the dark forests of Mount Noble. The mountain had always seemed a bit frightening to Daniel, constantly looming over their heads, but the lights of Noble's Green glowed warmly in the dark. They looked like home.

"Here," said Eric. "We're over Briarwood now. Let's take a little detour and I'll show you where I live."

Though he'd never been there, Daniel knew that Briarwood was a working-class neighborhood and it was a bit rougher than other parts of town. Though he didn't know why, he was surprised to find that Eric lived there. He had always assumed that Eric lived on a street like Elm Lane.

Eric flew lower, and soon the little lights became streetlamps and bedroom windows. The houses in Briarwood were smaller than those on Elm, but clean. The residents obviously took care of their neighborhood.

"That's my street over there," said Eric, pointing. "And my house is the third one down, and that's my mom's station wagon in the drive—"

Eric stopped in midsentence. They were no longer flying;

they were hovering now, suspended in midair. Eric's eyes were on a blue four-door Chevy parked next to the beaten-up old station wagon.

"Is . . . is there something wrong?" asked Daniel. It was a bit unnerving to be floating that far up without moving. It was less like flying and a lot more like hanging on.

"Huh?" said Eric. "Oh yeah. I'm fine, it's just . . . well, that car wasn't there when I left. It's Bob's."

"Is he . . . uh, Bob . . . is he your stepdad or something?"

"No!" answered Eric with such conviction that Daniel had to tighten his grip. "He's just my mom's boyfriend. Her latest. Or at least he was. He left last week and I was hoping that he was gone for good."

Daniel didn't say anything. He didn't think there was anything to say.

"Aw, the heck with him," Eric said finally. "C'mon, let's get you home."

They flew in silence for the next few minutes. Finally Eric's scowl broke as he spotted something near the edge of town.

"Well, look at that!" he exclaimed. "You mind if we make a quick stop? There's something I should take care of."

Daniel tried to make out what Eric was looking at, but it was no use. Whatever Eric was seeing, it was too far away for Daniel's eyes.

"Uh, sure. What's up?"

"Unfinished business." Eric smiled as he began their descent.

When they got closer, Daniel could make out stacks of hollowed-out cars and rusty metal appliances—refrigerators, washers, ovens and the like. They were landing in the middle of an old junkyard near the edge of the forest. Piles of rusted metal and torn-up furniture littered the area. To their right was a twelve-foot-high chain-link fence hanging limp around a gaping hole. It looked as if a Mack truck had plowed a hole clean through it. From somewhere close by came the crash of smashing, squeaking metal: the sound of destruction.

Daniel was wondering what business Eric could possibly have in a place like this when a sudden breeze brought him the answer. The already unpleasant stink of the junkyard was now accentuated with the familiar stench of trouble.

"Lemme guess: Clay and Bud?" asked Daniel, waving at the foul air in front of his face.

"Yep. This place is their favorite hangout. We've got the tree house, they've got their junkyard. Kinda fits, don't you think?"

Eric must have noticed the look on Daniel's face because he smiled and winked. "Just stay close to me and you'll be fine."

"But . . . ," Daniel began, searching for the right words. "Are you sure? I mean, there *are* two of them. . . ."

"Trust me, Daniel. Clay's the only real danger. Bud's just a sidekick. I know how to handle this."

Though Eric landed lightly, it took Daniel a moment to get his land legs again. As Eric strode confidently toward the sounds of mayhem, Daniel struggled to keep up. What else could he do? He couldn't exactly fly away, and since he had no idea where this place was in relation to his house, walking home was also out of the question.

They found Clay standing on the hood of a rusted-out truck, clubbing the windshield with a bent fender. Bud stood some distance away, throwing bricks at the headlights. As it turned out, Bud was a pretty bad shot, and one brick went high, slamming into the back of Clay's skull.

"Watch it!" snarled Clay. The brick had split in two, but despite his growling, Clay had hardly flinched.

"Oh, that little brick didn't hurt you!" said Bud.

"You want me to throw it back, fatty? See how you like it?"

"All right! All right, I'm sorry."

The two bickered some more before returning to their random demolition. As he watched the senseless destruction, Daniel thought what a waste it was for two trouble-makers like Clay and Bud to have powers. And here was Daniel, as unremarkable as bread.

Eric stood by and watched the pair for a minute or two before stepping out of the shadows into the moonlight. By now Daniel's eyes had adjusted to the dark, but he still didn't like the idea of being left behind in this creepy place, so he pinched his nose and followed Eric into the open.

"Uh-oh," said Bud, seeing Eric's approach. "Clay, man. Look out."

Clay looked up from his work and glared when he saw

Eric walking toward him. Daniel's feeling of unease was only made worse when Clay jumped off the beaten-up car to meet Eric head-on. Daniel's gut tightened when he noticed that Clay didn't drop the fender.

"Well. Looks like the new kid's making more friends every day. The Buddha and the girlie weren't enough, huh?"

"Clay, it's time we had a talk," said Eric.

"That so? Isn't it a little late for you to be out on a school night, Boy Scout?"

Bud was laughing along with Clay's taunts, but Daniel suspected it was only to cover his fear; the air had taken on a more pungent tang.

"I'm serious, Clay," said Eric, unsmiling. "What you did to Daniel here was way over the line. He could've died!"

"Hey, it's not my fault that yellowbelly over there went jumping offa that building! All I was gonna do was talk to him and he went all crazy!"

"Talk? You're not much of a talker, Clay."

"Oh yeah? And who are you to say anything about it, anyway? I'm not a part of your little *clique,* your group of 'Supers' or whatever, and you can't tell me what to do!"

"You know the rules, Clay. And even you have to follow them. Consider this your last warning. Leave Daniel, and everyone else for that matter, alone. Stick to beating up on junk—it's what you're good at."

Eric turned around and started to walk away, which Daniel saw immediately was a giant mistake. As soon as his back was turned, Clay swung the fender, hard, with both hands. Daniel managed to shout a warning, but it wasn't necessary. Eric spun around just in time and stopped the fender inches from his face. Both boys were now holding on to opposite ends of the metal club, and Daniel could see the strain on their faces as each tried to wrest it away from the other.

The sound of twisting metal ground against his eardrums as Daniel watched the two boys tear the fender apart under their very fingers. It was amazing and frightening all at the same time—they were so strong that the steel was bending, ripping in their grasps. The struggle seemed evenly matched, and Daniel began to worry that Eric had overestimated his advantage. If Clay was just as strong, how could Eric be sure that he would win? And what if Bud got his courage up and decided to step in on Clay's side? Daniel was quick-witted, but he was pretty sure that a battle of wits was not what Bud had in mind.

Just then the fender broke and the two boys fell, each holding a twisted, ruined piece in his hand.

Clay regained his footing first and rushed headlong toward Eric. Eric got to his feet and braced himself for the impact, which was massive. Daniel's ears rang as Clay nearly knocked Eric off his feet. The boys were wrestling now, in a struggle to gain leverage over the other. Then, in a furious display of strength, Clay finally managed to get the upper hand, literally lifting Eric off the ground and throwing him across the yard.

Eric landed in a heap at Daniel's feet. He was battered

and bruised, and his clothes were muddy and torn, but despite it all, he managed to stand.

"Had enough, Clay?" he asked, spitting out a bit of blood and smiling.

Like a bull seeing red, Clay bellowed with rage and charged. But this time Eric did things differently. When Clay got close, Eric sidestepped and grabbed him with both hands—and flew. Up, straight up, carrying him high into the night sky, with Clay shouting and cursing all the way.

Just like that they were gone, and Daniel was left alone in the junkyard with Bud and his cloud of stink. Bud's laughter had stopped, and the fat bully seemed just as uncertain as Daniel about what to do next. The stink cloud was getting worse, though, nearly obscuring Bud from view as little strands of bad-smelling fog began to reach toward Daniel, almost as if they were seeking him out.

"Your power is a cloud of super-stink? Aw, c'mon!" said Daniel, pulling his shirt collar up over his nose and mouth.

He heard it before he saw anything—a distant sound, like someone whistling very far away. As it got louder, Daniel looked up and saw a shape hurtling toward the ground. Clay was falling out of the sky.

Daniel cringed to think what would happen when he hit the earth, and had barely a moment to wonder what had become of Eric when he saw him swoop in and grab Clay just seconds from impact. They circled the junkyard, with Clay clinging to Eric for life.

"Okay, here we go again," said Eric, and he started rising again, up into the dark.

"NO! NO! I GIVE!" shouted a terrified Clay. "I give!"

Eric changed direction and gently settled back onto the ground. Clay had turned white, and his windblown hair was sticking up on the top of his head. Daniel thought he saw a dead moth or two stuck among his curls. The kid looked ready to kiss the ground.

"So?" asked Eric.

"I'm . . . I'm sorry, Daniel. It won't happen again," said Clay through clenched teeth. Of all the apologies Daniel had heard in his life, this one sounded the weakest. But it was enough for him.

"Bud, you're getting a pass this time, but the same goes for you," said Eric. "Leave Daniel alone." There was no answer from the stink cloud, but Daniel knew he had heard. Bud was like an ostrich with his head in the sand, just hoping for the two of them to go away.

"C'mon, Daniel, it's late."

Daniel grabbed hold of Eric's back and up they flew, leaving the two bullies to their shame.

After they were out of earshot, Daniel said, "Thanks for that."

"No problem. Clay's strong, he's incredibly tough, but he's not a flier. Probably for the best, since he's scared of heights." Eric winked. "Can't imagine why."

Then came that laugh—Eric's contagious laugh—but this time Daniel didn't share the smile. Clay was a bully, it was true, and he might even be truly dangerous, but nevertheless Daniel couldn't shake the image of Clay's genuinely terrified face as he fell.

Daniel wondered—just how powerful was Eric? Did he even know? Was there any limit to the things he could do? And what did that mean—for so much power to be in the hands of a twelve-year-old boy?

Chapter Seven
Hide-and-Seek

No matter how powerful Eric was, he couldn't help where it really mattered—he couldn't help Daniel's gram.

Over the next month, as Daniel's friendships with the Supers grew tighter, Gram seemed to be getting weaker. These days, more often than not, she didn't even get out of bed. She still went to the doctor's office every three weeks for her chemotherapy, but other than that she didn't leave the house. The treatment was almost as hard on her as the cancer itself. And though Gram smiled through it all and claimed that strong medicine was the best kind, Daniel wasn't so sure.

But she still lit up when Daniel came to her room, and he

made sure that he spent time with her every day. She still laughed and told jokes, and she made fun of her bald head when the chemo made her hair fall out (she said that if she had known what a nicely shaped head she had, she would've shaved it years ago). Daniel's mother bought her an assortment of scarves and hats to wear if she felt like it. But though her spirits were up, Daniel noticed that she was sleeping more and more—she had bags under her eyes that never went away.

When he couldn't be with Gram, Daniel relished his time with his friends at the tree fort. His favorite game (because it was the one he was best at) was hide-and-seek.

Daniel used to think that hide-and-seek was a game for little kids, but that was before he played it with the Supers. He was a decent hider, and the tree fort and surrounding woods offered plenty of hiding spots. But his real skill was being It. The rules were simple—the hiders had to make it back to base (the fort) without being discovered by the person who was It. Powers were allowed, but fliers had to stay below the tree line and there could be no physical contact of any kind. In the first game Rohan was It, and though everyone assumed he'd be great at this role, he was actually kind of lousy. Rohan's powers were all about his heightened senses, but that also meant that he was easily distracted. If he tried to sniff someone out, he was likely to get overwhelmed by a blooming rosebush half a mile away. Rohan's turn was over fast.

Daniel was up next. He spotted Louisa, Rose and Rohan

right away, and now all that was left was Simon and the two fliers. Because of her invisibility powers, Rose might have been nearly impossible to find, but luckily she got a case of the giggles whenever she tried to hide.

"Just three left," said Rohan, sitting on a nearby stump. "Think you can do it?"

"Of course he can," said Louisa. "He found you fast enough, didn't he?"

"That's only because Chuckles here wouldn't stop following me around."

Rose materialized next to him. "I don't like to hide alone. I get scared!"

Daniel let the three of them argue. His attention was on Simon, Eric and Mollie. The trick now was to outwait them. He couldn't match any of them in power, but if they got bored, they might get careless.

Daniel took a seat next to Rohan and waited. He sat there for at least fifteen minutes. Behind him, Rose was singing a little song of her own creation about hiding and seeking, while Rohan stared off into space, lost in a world only he could see. Louisa smiled at Daniel whenever he looked her way, so he resolved not to.

After a while longer, a voice from the trees grumbled, "Aw, to heck with this!" Daniel felt his head start to tingle and turned around just in time to see a tiny ball of static electricity, no bigger than a penny, explode just inches from his nose.

"Ow! Simon! You're out!"

"Yeah, I know, but the look on your face was worth it! Besides, my butt's asleep."

"And next time, I'd appreciate it if you'd keep your little wisps away from my face."

"Man, Corrigan! It was just a little shock. You are *such* a girl!"

Daniel turned his back on Simon—it was useless arguing with that kid.

Four down—that left only Eric and Mollie.

Daniel wasn't surprised that it had come down to the two fliers. They were probably floating somewhere above his head, hidden in the leaves, just waiting to make their move. But there was something that Daniel had noticed about fliers—they never thought about *not* flying; they never considered that sometimes it might be a better idea to just *walk*. No, they would definitely be airborne, which meant that he didn't need to worry about looking down. Up was all he had to be concerned with.

Another fact about those two was that they were very competitive. Always racing each other, always showing off . . .

"Hey, guys," Daniel said, loud enough for everyone to hear. "Tell you what: Let's make it more interesting. Let's make a side bet—whoever gets to base first can have my dessert at lunch for the next week. No, let's say for a month! That is, if you're fast enough . . ."

"No contest!" said Simon. "Eric's going to cream Mollie! She doesn't have a chance this time."

"Nuh-uh," sang Rose. "Mollie's fastest. She's the best flier and everyone knows. Michael was once but now it's Mollie."

This was perfect, thought Daniel. Fuel to the fire.

Then he heard it—a rustle of wind accompanied by a swooshing sound coming from the treetops. Then another, from the other direction. They were stirring up a breeze, they were flying so fast, both aiming for the same target. . . .

"Uh-oh," said Louisa. "I can't watch. . . ."

Louisa's words disappeared in a small thunderclap overhead, and when it cleared, Eric and Mollie were lying on the ground, dazed and startled. Leaves and debris were flying everywhere in the fallout of their midair collision.

"Ow!" said Mollie, sitting up. "You should really watch where you're going."

"Says you," answered Eric.

Daniel strutted over to where the two of them were sitting, rubbing their heads and looking sheepish but otherwise unhurt.

"Go on, Daniel," said Eric. "Say it."

"Eric and Mollie—you're out. *And* I'll be keeping my desserts, thank you very much."

"All right, but this time I get to be It," said Mollie, brushing the leaves off her backside.

"This game is a bore," whined Simon. "Let's do something fun for a change."

"Like what?" asked Daniel. "Play Simon Shocks all afternoon? No thanks."

"Quiet, everyone!" said Rohan. "I'm trying to concentrate."

They did as they were told. Rohan rarely raised his voice and when he did, everyone knew that he wasn't fooling around.

Eric walked over to him and quietly asked, "What's up? You see something?"

"No, but I think I smell smoke. I definitely smell smoke. A lot of it. Something's on fire and I don't hear any fire trucks."

Eric was all action.

"Okay, then, game's over. Rohan, I'll fly—you navigate. And, Simon, you're with us, too. We need to hurry."

"I wanna go!" said Rose.

"No," answered Eric. "You're too young, Rose. You know that."

"But we can't leave her here alone," said Louisa. "Maybe I should stay here with her."

"We might need your phasing powers, Louisa. But you're right, she can't stay here alone." Eric scratched his chin and looked around. "Hey, Daniel! You can watch Rose, right? We'll be back as soon as we can."

"Guys," said Rohan, with that faraway look on his face, "we need to hurry. . . ."

Eric looked pleadingly at Daniel. What else was Daniel going to do? He wouldn't be any help putting out a fire, anyway. He'd probably just get in the way.

"Yeah, of course," he answered. "You guys just get going. Rose'll be fine with me."

"Great! Thanks, man!"

Louisa stepped up and gave Daniel an unexpected kiss on the cheek. "I know she'll be in good hands, Daniel."

Mollie stamped her foot. "Let's go, already!"

Louisa took Mollie's hand, and Daniel watched as the rest of her body phased into her ghost form. She left her hand solid so that she could hold on, but with the rest of her body incorporeal she weighed next to nothing. As Mollie lifted off the ground, carrying the featherlight Louisa, Daniel could even see flecks of dust passing through Louisa's body in the sunlight.

Rohan climbed onto Eric's back and Simon wrapped his arms around Eric's waist. Daniel was worried that Eric wouldn't be able to fly with that much extra weight, but he took off after Mollie with no problem whatsoever.

As the Supers disappeared past the trees, Daniel felt his earlier euphoria disappear along with them. He might be good at games but when it came to real heroics, he was useless. At times like this he was, at best, a convenient babysitter.

And to make matters worse, when he looked, Rose was now nowhere to be found. Was it possible that they had been gone all of a few seconds and Daniel had already lost her?

"Rose?" he called. "Rose, where are you?"

He heard a small, giggly voice answer him from not too far away. "Come and find me!"

Daniel took a deep breath and let it out in a long, depressed sigh. While the rest of his friends were off saving lives, he was stuck here, playing hide-and-seek with the Invisible Little Girl.

Chapter Eight
Moon-Gazing

"**Y**ou know, I totally could have gone in there and saved that baby."

"Oh yeah? What would you have done? Shocked the fire away? Your wisps are suddenly fire-retardant?"

"All I'm saying is that I could have done more if Mr. Superhero here would've let me."

"Eric just acted on instinct!"

"Mollie . . ."

"No, it's true."

"Well, we *all* did our part. Good job, team."

"I was scared, Eric."

"So was I, Louisa. But you didn't let your fear get the better of you. You did good."

". . . All I'm saying is that if you had run into a terrorist or some kind of alien bounty hunter in there, you would've totally needed my help."

"Of course, Simon. Of course."

Daniel and the Supers were sitting in Rohan's backyard, looking for shooting stars. Or at least Rohan and Daniel were looking for shooting stars. The rest were replaying the events of the big fire—apparently, a house near the edge of town had caught fire and the mother almost died from the smoke. When they got there, Eric rushed in and saved a two-year-old baby, then went back in for the unconscious mother. When the fire trucks arrived, she and her baby were both sitting on the grass, safe. The Supers were nowhere around.

"Okay, looking for these shooting stars is the lamest of Daniel's many, many lame ideas," said Simon. "I'm going home to play Demolition Raceway."

"I'm having a good time," said Louisa, barely stifling a yawn. "But it is getting kind of late . . . it's past Rose's bedtime." Rose was snoring softly in Louisa's lap.

"It was fun, though, Daniel," she said. "I'd do it again!"

"Thanks, Louisa," answered Daniel. "I'm sorry, guys. They said there would be a big meteor shower tonight. Maybe it's just too cloudy down here."

"Don't sweat it, Daniel," said Eric. "We'll see them next time around. Race you home, Mollie?"

Eric turned but Mollie was already up in the air.

"You're toast!" she shouted, disappearing into the distance.

"Darn it," said Eric, calling after her, "give me half a chance, why don't you. . . ."

The rest of them waved goodbye as they got on their bikes. Daniel looked over at his friend, but Rohan's attention was focused intently on one part of the sky. The two of them were alone now and it had gotten very quiet. It was a nice change.

"Whatcha looking at?"

"There," said Rohan, pointing. "See, the moon's rising."

"Oh yeah. I can see it."

"Not like I can."

Daniel mulled this over for a minute. He knew his friend could see things at far distances, but the moon was hundreds of thousands of miles away.

"You mean you can see all that way? Details and everything?"

"Yep."

"Then how come you wear glasses?"

"I'm farsighted. I need these for reading."

"So you can see craters on the surface of the moon, but you need your glasses to read a book?"

"Yep."

"That's weird."

"Yeah, well."

Daniel smiled and looked back at the night sky. The waxing moon hung low in the sky like a sliver, barely a fingernail to Daniel's eyes.

"So . . . what's it look like? To you, I mean."

"Remember the star show we saw at the planetarium?" Rohan asked, his eyes never leaving the sky. "Those pictures they took with the big telescope?"

"Yeah."

"Well, I don't need a telescope. Right now I am looking at the Sea of Tranquility."

"There's a sea on the moon? You're nuts."

"It's not a real sea. It's just what they call it. It's actually a huge desert where the sand never shifts, never moves—because, of course, there isn't any wind on the moon."

"Spooky," said Daniel.

"Kind of. But it's beautiful, too."

"Rohan?"

"Yeah?"

"Do you ever get afraid of losing your powers? Afraid of . . . you know, what happens when you turn thirteen?"

"Sure I do," answered Rohan. "We all do, but there's nothing we can do about it. It's going to happen to all of us, no matter what Mollie says."

"Mollie? What does Mollie say?"

Rohan sighed. "Mollie's one of my best friends, but she's a troublemaker. She's always questioning the Rules, especially that one. The Third Rule: It Ends at Thirteen. She just won't accept that some good things are destined to come to an end."

"But you do? You can just accept that when you turn thirteen, you'll lose . . . all of this?"

"Eric believes that we can change our future by doing good deeds now. He thinks that, like Johnny Noble, we can grow up and become superheroes or something. I think that it's a nice thought, and it sure would be great if that were true. . . ."

"But . . . ," said Daniel.

"My family believes in duty, Daniel. And I know the rest of you make fun of me for being a 'good kid,' but I can't help it; it's who I am. I think we've been given these powers for a reason, and the trade-off is to be responsible and follow the Rules. To do our duty.

"Maybe it's just our destiny to give up our powers when we turn thirteen," said Rohan, finally taking his eyes off the bright moon. "You can't fight fate, Daniel. And you won't be happy as long as you keep trying."

Daniel looked at his friend in a whole new way. Rohan had always seemed a little strange, what with his tiny ties and loafers, but now he seemed . . . almost wise.

"Wow," said Daniel. "Maybe you should have Mollie over for dinner sometime, explain all that to her."

"It would never work," answered Rohan. "Mollie hates curry."

Daniel laughed and Rohan said good night as he went inside. As Daniel pulled his Windbreaker tight around his neck, a voice startled him from the dark.

"Hey, New Kid."

Daniel looked up to see Mollie standing by the edge of the yard.

"Oh, hey," answered Daniel. "I didn't see you there."

"That's 'cause I just got here," said Mollie, pointing to the sky.

"Oh, got it," said Daniel. *Man, she really is fast.* "Thought you were headed home?"

Mollie wrinkled her nose. "I wasted Eric and then got bored. Thought I'd see if you guys were still here."

"Oh. Well, I was just heading home, actually."

"Cool. I'll walk with you."

Daniel did a quick double take, surprised. Mollie usually had only the bare minimum of contact with him, and this was certainly the first time she'd offered to spend time with him alone. He was immediately suspicious.

They walked together in silence for the first few minutes. Daniel didn't understand why he always found it so hard to talk to Mollie, but it had something to do with the way she looked at him—as if she was examining him, or waiting for him to do or say something. Whatever it was, it was about as much fun as watching Georgie clap.

Daniel decided to use this opportunity to say something he had been meaning to say for a long time.

"I never thanked you."

Mollie made a face. "You never thanked me for what?"

"That first day, when we were moving in. You saved Georgie from being hit by that car."

Mollie just shrugged. "It was no big deal."

"Yes, it was! And I didn't even see you do it! Are you really that fast?"

This made Mollie smile a bit. "When I need to be—yeah, I'm that fast."

"Well, anyway. I just wanted to say thanks. I should've said it a long time ago."

Mollie chewed on her lip. It looked as if she was thinking something over. "Why don't we just say that you owe me one?"

"Sure. Deal."

They walked a little farther without saying anything more. Daniel decided that talking was certainly better than silence, so he tried to strike up a little more conversation.

"Boy, Rohan sure sucks at hide-and-seek."

"Tell me about it. He's too busy listening to the leaves grow or some other weird thing."

Daniel laughed. "Yeah, but at least he's not a jerk like Simon. The hair on the top of my head's still singed!"

Mollie stopped walking. "Just lay off Simon, okay?"

"I didn't mean anything by it," he muttered.

"You don't know anything about anything, New Kid." Mollie suddenly bristled with anger.

Daniel had had enough. "What is that supposed to mean? All I said was that Simon can be a jerk sometimes, because it's true! How many times have I gotten shocked in the face for no reason? And why you go out of your way to defend him when you are such a pain to everyone else, especially me . . ."

"It's Simon's birthday next week," she said.

"So what? Does that mean you'll be nice to me when *my* birthday comes around?"

Mollie turned to Daniel and he was shocked to see tears in her eyes. But the tears didn't stop her from shouting, "Don't you get it? He's turning thirteen! We are all being nice to Simon because in a week we won't even know him anymore!"

Daniel was stunned. He'd never even wondered about Simon's age before. Now he knew.

"Oh," he said. "I'm . . . I'm sorry." What else was there to say?

Mollie rubbed at her eyes, angrily brushing away the tears that had pooled there.

"Michael was the last one, and he was my best friend. He was the best flier there ever was, and then one morning he just wakes up and forgets it all! He was so determined not to, he even wrote himself notes, he drew pictures, so that he would remember, but it didn't work. Nothing ever works. He stopped hanging out with us right after that. Now, at school, he doesn't even look at me. Eric and Rohan will tell you that it's just the way things are, that we all need to accept it. But that's not true. Something bad happens when we turn thirteen, and I won't just *accept it*!"

Daniel didn't know what to say. After all, if it had been him with those powers, he would never want to be ordinary, not ever.

Mollie had calmed down somewhat and was done shouting. But she hadn't let go of her anger, either, Daniel could tell. She was simply holding it back, keeping it in check.

"And you know who's next after that, don't you?" she asked.

Daniel shook his head, but he could guess.

"Eric," she answered. "And you know what this town will be like without him? What *Clay and Bud* will be like? Without Eric around, no one can stop Clay. He's just too strong . . . too strong."

Daniel wondered whom she was trying to convince, him or herself. "Mollie, why are you telling me all this? Why are you even hanging out with me? I'm sorry for what's going to happen to Simon, I really am, but it's obvious you don't like me, so why are we here?"

"Because you're the only one, Daniel," she said, looking at him again. "You're the only one who can break the Third Rule. Forever." Mollie wore an expression he had never seen on her before, one that was almost worse than the anger, worse because it was directed at him. It was hope.

"You're the only one who can save us."

Daniel was stunned, and he was pretty sure that Mollie was crazy. If the Supers of Noble's Green couldn't stop whatever was happening to them, what could he do?

"But how? I'm nothing special."

"And that's why you're perfect. See, I have this plan. And it'll work. So shut up, walk and listen. . . ."

The next day at school, Daniel managed to avoid Mollie— and all of the Supers for that matter. What would he say to them? Did Mollie expect him to lie for her? Though he hadn't yet made up his mind, he was very close to doing so.

What Mollie wanted from him was very simple and also very frightening.

Mollie suspected you didn't just wake up on your birthday without powers—something had to take them away. And she wasn't alone in her suspicions. Eric had told her a story once about a couple of Supers who decided to try and save their friend. On the night before his thirteenth birthday, they stayed over at his house. The plan had been to stay awake with him all night, to keep a watch over him and to keep him safe. But when the three friends emerged from the house the next morning, all three were the same—ordinary. Even though two of the friends were only twelve at the time, they had undergone the same transformation. Because they had tried to save their friend, whatever had taken his powers had also come for theirs.

No one had tried anything like it since.

This was where Daniel came into the picture. Since he had no powers to start with, he was in no danger of losing them. He could stay with Simon, and at the very least bring back information about what really happened on a Super's thirteenth birthday. At best, he might actually be able to stop it.

Him. Daniel Corrigan.

"Hey, anyone sitting here?"

Daniel looked up from his lunch of tuna fish and crackers

and saw a boy standing over him with a lunch tray. He was a little older than Daniel, and though they had never spoken, Daniel knew him very well. Rohan had pointed him out several times.

The boy was Michael, who, once upon a time, had been the best flier there ever was.

"Uh, no," answered Daniel. "Go right ahead."

"So, you're new, aren't you?" he asked, sitting down across from Daniel.

"Yeah, sort of. My family moved here in August, just before school began."

"You like it?"

Daniel thought for a moment about all that he had seen and heard in just a few months—the exhilaration of flight, the cold fear of finding himself alone with Clay and Bud—things he'd never dreamed would happen to him.

"I like it a lot."

"That's good," said Michael, without much enthusiasm.

It was strange to be sitting here talking to Michael after all he had heard about him. It reminded him of the first time he saw Gram after finding out that she was sick. He hadn't known then what to say or what to do, and he'd been terrified of saying or doing the wrong thing. Looking at Michael, Daniel felt the same way.

They ate without saying much of anything while Daniel tried not to stare. It was hard for him, though—he wanted to examine Michael's every move, to see if he acted the same as the other Supers. Did he move differently or talk differently? Daniel wondered if the signs would be visible if you knew what to look for.

"So I've seen you hanging around Eric and Mollie and those guys," said Michael out of the blue. "Are you friends with them?"

"Sure, I guess."

"That's good. They're cool kids. You know, I used to hang out with them until . . . until . . ."

Michael seemed to be struggling to find the right word.

"Well, I guess I just got too old . . . or something."

"Too old?"

"Huh? I dunno, I guess we just . . . got interested in different things."

"Oh," said Daniel. "I guess that happens."

"They just wanted to keep playing the same dumb games, you know? The same stuff that we did when we were little kids, and, I don't know, it just seemed silly all of a sudden."

Michael stared at his food, but he was no longer eating.

"How's Mollie these days?" he asked.

"She's fine, I guess."

"Boy, me and Mollie, we used to race each other all the time . . . I think . . . to see who was the fastest . . . runner, I guess. I don't really remember. It's strange, you'd think I'd be able to."

Michael rubbed his eyes with his palms, as if he were trying to wipe the sleep away.

Daniel decided to try something then, something he knew was reckless but still worth a shot.

"Mollie's told me about that," he said. "She said that you two would race to see who was the fastest . . . flier."

"Wh-what was that?" Michael looked Daniel in the eyes for the first time since sitting down, and a change came over his face. Michael seemed close to something now, very close, but it was still just out of view.

Daniel leaned in and whispered, "I know all about it, Michael. I know that you flew! They say that you were the best flier there ever was! Even Mollie says so. Can't you remember?"

Michael was speaking slowly now, and he shut his eyes tight.

"I . . . remember . . . the wind. . . ."

Just then his eyes popped back open and he started as if someone had just poured a bucket of ice water over his head.

"I used to dream a lot," he said, suddenly relaxed. "I dreamt that I could fly. Almost every night. But I haven't had that dream in a long, long time."

Without another word, Michael stood and walked off. He didn't bother with his lunch tray and he didn't say goodbye to Daniel, or even acknowledge that they had been talking. He just wandered away, slowly, into the crowd of kids milling about the cafeteria, kids who were worried about other boys, girls, grades and parents. Kids with ordinary worries, kids who were just like him.

Watching him disappear into the crowd, Daniel knew what he would do. His mind was made up, and he had Michael to thank for that.

Chapter Nine
Simon's Birthday

Daniel soon discovered that when Mollie said she had a plan, what she really meant was *I have this kinda general idea of something that should happen, so you go and make it work.* Mollie Lee was brave. Mollie Lee was persistent. Mollie Lee was not, however, a detail person.

The first part of the plan was secrecy. Daniel didn't like lying to Eric and Rohan, but Mollie convinced him that if they found out, Rohan would scold them and Eric might go so far as to try and stop them. As Mollie had said before, those two believed in the Rules and they didn't hold with anyone breaking them.

So after much debate, Daniel and Mollie decided that the

only members of their little conspiracy would be those who needed to know: the two of them, of course, and Simon. Daniel was surprised by Simon's reaction when they finally clued him in to what they had planned. Far from being grateful for the risk Daniel was about to take, he seemed to resent that Daniel had to be involved at all. He acted as if it were a great inconvenience to have Daniel stay with him on the night before his birthday, and laid down a ridiculous number of rules (Daniel could stay in his room but he wasn't allowed to touch any of his stuff—that sort of thing). At one point Daniel was ready to call the whole thing off, until Mollie quietly reminded him that they weren't only doing this for Simon, they were doing it for Eric, too.

Mollie wanted to be involved, but they decided that she needed to keep a safe distance away. She would camp out in a pup tent in the woods next to Simon's house (her parents thought that she was sleeping over at Louisa's). From there, she could keep an eye on Simon's bedroom window without actually putting herself in jeopardy. Or so they hoped. Daniel argued for Mollie to stay at her own house, far away from any risk, but Mollie stubbornly refused. The pup tent was the best compromise they could come up with.

As for Daniel, he was left with the near-impossible task of packing. On the afternoon before Simon's thirteenth birthday, Daniel stood in his room staring at the pile of junk that he'd spread out over his bed. After all, what do you pack for guarding a superpowered kid? He'd decided that overkill was his best bet: one flashlight, extra batteries, a two-liter bottle of soda (to help him stay awake), a book of Holmes stories (to help pass the time if nothing happened), a whistle (to call for help if something did happen), a bag of beef jerky, a compass, some rope, an instant camera, his magnifying glass and an extra pair of underwear (just in case).

"I thought you were going to a sleepover. Where's your friend live, the bottom of a well?"

Daniel was startled by the thin voice from over his shoulder. When he turned around, he was surprised to see Gram standing in the attic doorway.

"Gram? Aren't you supposed to be in bed?"

"Oh, pshaw!" she said, making a face. "I'm tired of looking at the same four walls all day long. Need to get my blood moving."

But Daniel could hear the exhaustion in her voice, the crackle in her lungs that sounded like paper, and he noticed the way she leaned into his door frame for support. The simple trip up the stairs had taken every bit of extra strength she had.

He quickly brushed his pile of junk aside and made a space for her on his bed. "Here, Gram, sit down."

"Well, don't mind if I do. Just while I catch my breath."

She sat down heavily on the edge of his bed. It was a slow process, careful and deliberate. These days she always moved like that, as if she were made of glass in a house full of hard edges.

When she'd settled, she gave a satisfied thump of her cane and gestured toward the gear strewn all over Daniel's bed.

"So, is this what kids do for fun these days?" She fingered the coil of rope suspiciously. "Planning to tie someone up and force-feed them beef jerky and soda all night long?"

Daniel smiled, but he could feel a tight ball of guilt winding up in his stomach—he didn't like having to lie to her. Not to Gram.

"It's just stuff," he said. "We were thinking about camping out in Simon's yard."

Gram's eyes narrowed as she mulled this over. "Well, you be careful, then. There's a whole lotta forest around here, and you wouldn't be the first child to be carried off in the middle of the night by rabid raccoons. They grow big in these parts, you know."

Daniel laughed. "I'll be extra careful."

"By the way, I hear you met little Mollie Lee from across the street. Such a sweetheart. A real cutie, too. Don't you think?"

At the mention of Mollie, the ball in Daniel's stomach did a small, unexpected flip. Why was Gram smiling?

"She's okay," he said quickly. "For a girl, I mean. She's fun to hang out with. Actually, she's more like a boy in a lot of ways. . . ."

Why was it so stuffy in here?

"Well," continued Gram, "I remember when she was just a chubby little thing in pigtails and frilly dresses. The poor girl's mother tried for years to dress her like one of those porcelain dolls, but it never looked right on Mollie. She dirtied up more beautiful dresses. . . . Eventually her parents must've just given up."

Daniel smiled at the thought of Mollie wearing a frilly anything. "Can't say I blame them," he said. "When Mollie gets her mind set on something, that's the end of it."

"You don't say? And what's she got her mind set on these days?"

Another stomach jump. Just what was Gram getting at?

"Nothing. I mean, she's always on about something or other, but it's never a big deal. Girl stuff, you know?"

Gram nodded and rested her chin on her hands as she twirled her cane between her fingers. Her bent shape was silhouetted against the attic window, and just over her shoulder Daniel could see the sun drooping low over the trees. In the pink evening glow she looked as she had before the cancer—rosy and full of health.

"I'm glad that you're making friends, Daniel. I know that coming here couldn't have been easy on you—a new town, a new school. There's a lot of grown-up stuff going on here with my being sick and all, but I don't want you to forget to be a kid—at least for a little while longer."

Daniel nodded.

"This was my room when I was little," she continued, her gaze far away. "Did you know that? Oh sure, this house has been around for a long, long time. Much longer than this old lady. I remember staring out that window at Mount Noble for what must have been hours at a time. I'd stare at the clouds and the sky, and the stars at night. You know, as you get older the gray matter starts to fail on you and your memories get all fuzzy—they disappear into mist. I don't remember much from my childhood, but I do remember staring out that window and dreaming. I bet I had wonderful dreams. . . ."

She reached over and pinched Daniel on the arm. Her eyes looked a little moist, but Daniel couldn't be sure in the fading light.

"Don't grow up too fast, Daniel. No matter what else happens, promise me that."

"I promise, Gram," he said. "I promise."

And he meant it.

Later that night, Daniel was forced to sit through an awkward dinner with Simon's family. He basically had to pretend that he and Simon were best buddies, which was nearly impossible to do when Simon was actually around. Throughout the meal, Simon took advantage of every opportunity to make a joke at Daniel's expense. Daniel had never been a fan of pork chops, and when he didn't clean his plate, Simon laughingly accused him of "watching his figure for Mollie." Daniel wanted to tell Simon to shut his fat little face, but since he was sitting at Simon's dinner table, he was forced to grin and bear it.

After dinner, the two boys were excused from the table and spent the rest of the evening in Simon's room. Simon was a speed freak (which Daniel thought was ironic, considering that he was an even slower runner than Daniel; his only power seemed to be creating those little electric wisps), and he had decorated his room with NASCAR posters and plastic models of sports cars. There were no books to be found, but plenty of video games—most of which involved racing. Just looking at his room, Daniel was reminded of how little the two of them had in common. They were two members of the same secret club who otherwise wouldn't give each other the time of day.

Still, for one night at least, they were stuck with each other.

Simon sat at the foot of his bed and untangled a video-game controller from a mass of wires. He started playing some kind of vehicle-demolition game, one in which his car seemed to earn points by repeatedly smashing into an ice cream truck. Daniel watched him play in silence for a few minutes.

"That your high score?" Daniel finally asked, trying to pass the time.

"Yeah," grunted Simon.

"So, what's the point of the game? Is there some kind of goal, or is it just about wrecking things or—"

"I'm just beating on Mr. Crazy Cream's truck to get enough power-ups to get to the next level. And you're not helping any by talking at me."

"Well, sorry. But what am I supposed to do all night while you play your game?"

"Not my problem."

That was it. Daniel was tired of Simon's smug attitude. If he didn't care about what happened, why should Daniel? They would find some other way to help Eric.

"You know what? Forget it! Just forget the whole thing! I'm going home."

"Who cares? You're not here to help me anyway; it's Eric you're all worried about."

Daniel felt a twinge of guilt. He probably should have seen it coming, but the truth was that he had never really considered Simon's feelings about all this.

"That's not true," said Daniel. "Mollie is worried about everybody. Even you."

"And what about *you*? Who are you doing this for?"

Daniel hesitated for a second before finally caving. "Fine. I'm doing this for Eric, and for Mollie. But it's not like you've ever even been nice to me. You're pretty much a jerk to everyone."

Simon threw his game controller to the ground. "That's because you're all such a bunch of losers!"

With that, Daniel picked up his backpack and headed for the door. This kid was unbelievable.

"Happy birthday," he said without turning around.

Daniel was just opening the door when a sound caught his attention: a sound he recognized but just couldn't believe he was hearing. Not from Simon, anyway.

He turned and watched as Simon wiped his nose on his

sleeve. His face was red and wet with tears. He wasn't just crying, he was bawling.

"Being . . . being scared stinks," he managed between sobs.

"Yeah," answered Daniel. "Yeah, it really does."

Daniel stood on the threshold for a moment or two, then slowly shut the door again. He put his backpack down on the floor, walked over and picked up the game controller.

"You got another one of these?" he asked.

A few hours later, they sat together keeping watch out the window. Every fifteen minutes one of them would aim a flashlight into the trees, flicking it on two times. Then Mollie's own light would shine back at them twice from her little campsite hidden in the woods, to signal that everything was normal. If one of them saw anything suspicious, they would hit the light three times. If there was immediate danger, they would flick the light on and off and keep it blinking until help arrived.

Once Simon's fear had broken through his bravado, he and Daniel had gotten along fine. Better than fine, actually—they had even managed to have fun. They played video games practically all evening, cracking each other up as they smashed their electronic cars and trucks into one another. They nearly made themselves sick on Daniel's beef jerky and soda. It turned out that Simon was a master burper and, with the aid of a little carbonation, could burp his way through the alphabet. It was only after Simon's mom poked her head in the door and informed them that it was bedtime, and therefore time for lights-out, that things got serious again.

The plan was to keep watch together at the window, communicating with Mollie in flashing, flickering lights. Daniel set up some of the equipment he'd brought—he wore his point-and-shoot camera around his neck and had his magnifying glass in his pocket. At one point, Simon gave him a baseball bat for protection, but Daniel just set it aside. He didn't know what they might end up facing, but he was pretty sure that a twelve-year-old armed with a baseball bat wouldn't do much good.

It was sometime after midnight when Simon spotted the shape in the dark.

Daniel was dozing, struggling to stay awake, when he realized Simon was tugging at his shirtsleeve.

"Look!" he whispered. "Over there by the streetlamp!"

Daniel jumped to his feet and squinted at the light shining beyond the trees. He searched the shadows.

"I don't see anything."

"Something was there a second ago."

Daniel immediately wished he had brought a pair of binoculars. He cursed himself for forgetting to pack something so obvious. Plenty of underwear, but no binoculars.

"You sure?" he asked. Maybe Simon's fear was getting the best of him.

"YES! I'm telling you, something is moving out there. . . . There! Look!"

Then Daniel saw it—two little specks of light moving through the darkness along the tree line. They were close together, reflecting an ambient glow, like a cat's eyes, but they were too high off the ground to belong to any cat. Whatever those eyes belonged to, it wasn't headed for Simon's house. It was moving away from them, into the trees.

"It's headed for Mollie!" whispered Simon.

Daniel grabbed the flashlight and flicked the on/off button three times. He waited. No response. He then started flicking the light rapidly, on and off, on and off. Still nothing.

The shining eyes were gone now, but Daniel had the sinking suspicion that whatever it was had moved deeper into the woods, and closer to Mollie.

"We've got to warn her," said Daniel. "Is there a way down from here?"

"The trellis, but you're crazy if you think I'm going out there!"

Daniel started to argue, until he saw the fear in Simon's eyes. The poor kid had been dreading this night for so long that now that it was here, he was petrified, nearly paralyzed with fear.

"All right, you stay here. If you see anything else, hit the flashlight!"

Then, against his better judgment, he swung his body out the window and slipped his feet and hands into the rails of the trellis. He had just started his descent when he heard Simon hiss at him. Daniel looked up to see Simon handing him the baseball bat through the window. This time, Daniel took it.

The grass was wet with dew, and Daniel nearly slipped on his butt running across the yard. If he hurried, he figured he could get to Mollie's camp from the other direction first, hopefully avoiding a confrontation in the dark with whatever it was in the woods. As he snuck along through the trees, he wondered at the ridiculousness of his situation—in a town full of child superheroes, what was he trying to do? Save the day?

I'm a moron, he almost said aloud.

He found Mollie's yellow pup tent in a clearing thirty yards into the woods, but there was no Mollie. The surrounding trees were thick and black in the moonlight. His heart was beating wildly in his chest as he realized that anything could be hiding just a few feet away and he wouldn't even see it.

He decided to chance a whisper. "Mollie? Mollie!"

"What?" answered an irritated voice from the bushes.

He spun around to see Mollie Lee trudging out of the brush, looking thoroughly peeved.

"What are you doing down here?" she asked.

"Me? What . . . Where were *you*? We shone the light but there was no answer!"

She scowled at him. "I had to go. Okay?"

"Go? Go where?"

"Just go!" Mollie's face was red and she sighed. "I had to *go*!"

"Oh," he said, feeling awkward.

"What are *you* doing—"

Mollie was cut off by the sound of something crashing through the brush. It was moving fast, no longer bothering with secrecy, and it was coming straight for them.

"Is that Simon?" she asked, turning toward the sound.

With no time to explain, and for reasons unknown even to him, Daniel found himself pushing Mollie behind him and stepping in front of whatever was about to appear. He brandished his bat high and shouted, "Mollie! Fly!"

But it was too late. He barely had time to get the words out before something slammed into him, knocking him off his feet with a loud "Umph!" There was a mass of flailing arms and legs, and something sticky was clinging to his face. A voice was shouting, "Get it off! Get it off!" but it didn't sound like his.

"Daniel, what are you doing? Let go of him!"

"Huh?" Daniel sputtered as he got his first good look at his opponent.

"Uh, hi?" said Rohan, under him. He was dirty and sweaty, but it was definitely Rohan. He was clawing at a spiderweb that clung to his face. The light from Daniel's flashlight reflected off Rohan's (now crooked) glasses in the dark.

The light reflected off his glasses in the dark, like two cat eyes moving through the trees. . . .

"Aw man," said Daniel. "It was you I saw from Simon's window."

"Rohan, what are you doing out here?" said Mollie, her hands on her hips. Then she turned on Daniel. "And what are *you* doing running around swinging a baseball bat? You're gonna hurt someone!"

Daniel stood up and offered Rohan his hand. The two boys wiped the dirt and leaves from their hair and looked at Mollie sheepishly.

"Well?" she asked.

"I thought he was a monster," said Daniel.

"Uh-huh," said Mollie. "And if he was, you were going to rush to my rescue armed with a *baseball bat*?"

"Yeah, I guess," said Daniel, wincing at the absurdity of his own bravery. He was prepared for one of Mollie's tongue-lashings, but to his surprise, she just looked at him. In a weird way.

"And you," she said finally, facing Rohan. "What are you doing here?"

Rohan was busy wiping his glasses on his shirttail. "I came to stop you. To try and talk some sense into you guys. I had no idea I'd be attacked by Slugger over there."

"What are you talking about?" Mollie asked, her face a mask. "We're just camping."

"Oh, come off it, Mollie! You guys have been acting all secretive and suspicious for days now. You two barely spoke until a week ago, and now you're on a campout together? And you just *happen* to pick the woods next to Simon's house, on the night before his thirteenth birthday?"

"You've been spying on us!" Mollie said, poking Rohan with her finger. "You used your powers and listened in, didn't you?"

"Of course I did, you dork! But only because I knew you were about to make a huge mistake!"

A thought struck Daniel like a hammer blow.

"Eric?" he asked. "Did you tell Eric?"

Rohan rearranged his glasses on his face and sighed, "No. But I should have. You guys are messing with things that are best left alone."

Mollie folded her arms across her chest. "Says you. I bet Simon sees it different."

"It's Simon's time, Mollie. And if you're not careful, you're going to end up just like him!"

Daniel was about to interrupt when he saw a light flicker through the trees.

"Oh shoot! It's Simon! He's gotta be crazy worried by now."

Daniel took Mollie's flashlight and switched it on twice, the signal for all clear.

The light from Simon's window flashed back—*one, two* . . .

"I should get back," said Daniel.

Three, four, five, six.

"Something's wrong," Mollie whispered.

The light was flashing on and off desperately.

"We've got to help him!" said Mollie as she started to move, but Rohan wrapped his arms around her tightly.

"Let go!" she screamed.

But Rohan held her firm. Mollie was fast and a flier, but she was no stronger than your average twelve-year-old girl. She couldn't shake Rohan loose.

"You can't go, Mollie!" said Rohan. "You'll end up just like him!"

Mollie was crying tears of frustration as she wrestled with her friend. "But what about Simon?" she pleaded.

Off in the distance was a sudden popping sound, like small firecrackers, and from Simon's window came the flashes of little balls of light. Simon's wisps.

"He's fighting back!" said Mollie.

"Daniel," said Rohan, "go!"

But Daniel was already running. In the distance he could hear Mollie shouting for him to hurry, and he ran as fast as he could. Branches scraped his face and thorns cut his legs as he sprinted through the underbrush, but he didn't dare slow down—he had made a friend tonight, and that friend was in trouble.

When he reached the trellis, the lightning from Simon's wisps had already ceased, and there was an eerie silence in the air, accompanied by the ozone smell of electricity. Daniel had been in such a hurry that he didn't remember to pick up the bat—all he had was the camera around his neck. Nevertheless, he climbed. His hands were shaking with fear, but somehow he managed to make them work, planting one after the other, as he scaled the wall to Simon's bedroom window.

It was dark inside, and through the open window Daniel smelled something new—a pungent odor, like burnt hair. As he peered over the ledge, a blast of cold air hit him in the face and he saw a hooded shape standing in the darkness. It was tall, like an adult, but only vaguely human-shaped. In the blackness of Simon's room, this figure stood out in its absence of light—a thing darker than the dark itself. It was a creature made of shadow except for a small, beating heart at the center of it—a faint green glow the size of a man's fist that pulsed with a sickly light. The creature had draped itself over Simon's inert body, which lay sprawled out over his bed. The whole shape of the thing seemed wrong somehow. It might have been an effect of the darkness, a trick of the eyes, but the shadow itself seemed to undulate; it rippled like waves on water. It chilled Daniel to his core and for some reason made him think of hundreds of night-black rats squirming in the dark.

As if reading his thoughts, the hooded thing turned and looked at him. At least it appeared to be looking at him—in the dark he couldn't make out any features, so he couldn't be sure that it really even had eyes. Daniel felt panic rising in his chest: he was alone and unarmed.

The shape drifted a step closer, and as it did, the unnatural cold got worse. The frozen air seemed to emanate from the shadow itself. Daniel did the only thing he could think of—he snapped a picture. The flashbulb exploded and his eyes danced with spots, but for a second at least, the figure paused. It regarded him silently and seemed interested in the camera in his hand. Daniel started back down the trellis, and had just taken his foot off the top rung when the shadow, sensing his retreat, rushed toward him. Daniel hit the camera button again.

Flash! Flash!

The bright camera bulb was making Daniel almost totally blind now, and he prayed that the flashes were having the same effect on the shadowy figure. He moved his foot down but missed the next rung. As he slid off the trellis, he reached out with his free hand, only to grab a fistful of air.

For a split second, Daniel dared to hope that Eric would be there, once more, to catch him. But there was no miraculous rescue this time, and the last thing he felt was his body hitting the wet grass and something breaking inside him. Then he felt nothing at all.

Chapter Ten
Welcome Guests

"Daniel, you've got some visitors here to see you. Are you feeling up to it, kiddo?"

"Yeah, of course. I keep telling you, Dad, I feel fine."

"Well, if you don't mind, I'll let the doctors make the diagnosis around here."

Frankly, Daniel felt anything but "fine." His right arm was throbbing with a dull ache that turned into a stabbing pain every time he moved it, and there was an itch halfway up his cast that was unreachable. At least the nausea was gone. This morning was the first time that he had been able to keep down a solid breakfast. That didn't make it taste any better, though. Hospital food was still hospital food.

Daniel heard someone cough and was surprised to see Rohan and Louisa standing in the doorway. When his dad had announced that he had his first visitors, he just assumed that Mollie would be among them.

"Hey," said Rohan. He was carrying a package under his arm, wrapped with metallic blue paper.

"Hey," Daniel said.

"Well," said Daniel's dad, grabbing his coat, "I'm going to go out and stretch my legs for a minute and let you kids catch up. No arm wrestling!"

The kids waited for Daniel's father to close the door behind him. Then Louisa sat down gently on the bed next to Daniel.

"Does it hurt?" she asked, eyeing the cast.

"A bit," answered Daniel. "But I've had worse."

Daniel caught Rohan rolling his eyes and Daniel felt himself blush. He hadn't had worse; he'd never so much as broken a finger before now. He didn't know why he was showing off in front of Louisa.

"I brought you some chocolates from the gift shop," she said. "I figured you'd be sick of the hospital food. All they had were the ones in the heart-shaped boxes. . . ."

"Uh, thanks," said Daniel.

"Okaaay," said Rohan. "So, Daniel? What's the prognosis? Do you get to keep missing school or are they finally kicking you out of here?"

"I'm leaving today or tomorrow. But I probably won't be back to school for another week."

"That's terrible," moaned Louisa. "We all miss you around the tree house.

"Oh, I almost forgot," she said, reaching into her coat pocket. "Rose wanted me to give you this."

She handed Daniel a crayon drawing of a boy—at least Daniel assumed it was supposed to be a boy—falling on his head. There was a happy yellow sun watching in the sky.

Daniel laughed. "Tell her thanks for me, Louisa. And tell her I plan on getting it framed."

"Do you need anything, Daniel?" she asked. "Do you need an extra pillow or anything?"

Daniel thought for a moment. "Well, I could go for a soda. If you don't mind."

Louisa practically leapt out of her shoes. "Sure! Is there a vending machine nearby?"

Rohan interjected before Daniel could answer, "Nope, you have to go all the way down to the cafeteria. All the way down on the ground floor."

"Oh, okay," said Louisa, blinking. "I'll be back in a few minutes, then."

She smiled at Daniel. "Don't go anywhere!"

Daniel gestured to his broken arm and smiled back. "I won't."

Rohan waited until Louisa was out of earshot, then turned back to Daniel.

"I think I've discovered your superpower, Daniel."

"Oh yeah?"

"You have the power to make Louisa swoon. It's kinda gross, actually."

"Me? But I—"

"Seriously," laughed Rohan. "Have you noticed the way she looks at you? You don't need super-senses to see it."

Daniel rolled his eyes, but the truth was that he *had* noticed. He just wasn't sure what he was supposed to think about it.

"Has Mollie said anything about her?"

Rohan adjusted his glasses and squinted at Daniel. "Mollie? No, why?"

"No reason," answered Daniel quickly. "It's just, you know . . . I'd never hear the end of it."

The two were silent for a moment before Daniel spoke up, more quietly this time. "How's Simon?"

"He's fine," answered Rohan. "Physically he wasn't hurt at all."

"That's a relief, but is he . . . does he . . ."

"He's just like all the others now. A *normal* thirteen-year-old boy."

Daniel's head sank back into his pillow. He caught the emphasis in Rohan's voice and understood immediately. So it had all been for nothing. Daniel had hoped that he had gotten to him in time—that he had stopped, or at least interrupted, whatever it was that . . . thing was trying to do. It would be hard to face Simon again, even though Daniel knew that he would have no memory of what had been done to him. But Daniel would know. He would never forget.

"So you broke your arm, huh?"

Rohan pulled a chair up next to his bed and began studying the control panel full of buttons that Daniel used to raise and lower the hospital bed.

"Yeah, and I had a pretty bad concussion. But I'm out of the woods, and I'm hoping to go home today. This place is dead-boring."

"Here, I brought you something. It might help pass the time." Rohan set the blue package on Daniel's lap. Daniel fumbled at the wrapper with his left hand, but he couldn't get the right leverage to tear the paper; it just kept sliding around on the sheets.

"Oh, sorry. Here, let me."

Rohan tore the paper off with a flourish and revealed a stack of Johnny Noble comics, each one bagged and boarded for extra protection.

"Wow. Are you sure?"

"Absolutely. Just don't get any pudding on them. This is strictly a Supers-loan. Since you can't go to the tree fort, I'm bringing the tree fort to you."

"Thanks, Rohan."

"Don't mention it." Rohan gestured to the panel next to the bed. "So, what do all these buttons do?"

"Don't touch them. Some move the bed up and down, and one of them calls the nurse. It took me, like, an hour to find the perfect position for this bed, so hands off!"

"Is your nurse pretty?"

"My nurse's name is Ralph."

"Oh. So . . . no?"

"No!" Daniel smiled in spite of himself, and Rohan looked pleased with his little joke. Things were suddenly easier between the two of them.

"So, have you talked to Mollie?" asked Daniel.

"Talked? No, not so much. Dodged—yes. At the bus stop she pretends I'm not even there, which was kind of a relief at first—at least she's no longer taking swings at me—but by now it's getting old."

"Daniel," Rohan went on, turning serious, "you know why I did it, right? Why I stopped her from helping?"

Daniel nodded.

Rohan continued, "She wouldn't have been able to help you. She would've ended up just like Simon."

"Yeah, I know. Mollie knows, too; that's probably why she's so mad at you right now. She hates it when other people are right."

"If it's any consolation, she gave me one heck of a black eye for my trouble." Rohan took off his glasses, and Daniel could see the faint outline of a yellow and blue bruise under Rohan's left eye. "You should have seen it a week ago. I looked like a prizefighter."

"A prizefighter who gets beaten by girls," Daniel teased.

"Well, yes. But mean girls. Very mean."

"Speaking of trouble—is Eric mad?"

"About what? As far as he knows, you were camping out with Mollie and me and you climbed the wrong tree."

"You mean . . . you lied to him?"

"I am withholding certain details of the truth until I get all the facts. There's no need to upset him until we know exactly what happened. And I was hoping you could tell me that. What happened at Simon's window? What'd you see, Daniel?"

And so Daniel recounted what he saw in Simon's bedroom that night—the darkness, the shadow that moved. Daniel was surprised at how hard it was to say it out loud for the first time, but he immediately felt better for having done it. Through it all, Rohan listened attentively, never interrupting, but Daniel did see his eyes go wide several times. It was affecting him, too. Rohan, who was always so calm, so unflappable, was afraid.

"I actually wondered if you saw anything, with your powers. I thought you might've . . ."

Rohan shook his head. "Trees were in the way. I can't see through things, you know. Plus, I was kinda busy getting punched in the face."

Rohan got up from his seat and started pacing the room.

"Proof. We need proof," he said.

"For what?"

"To convince Eric that what you saw wasn't simply your own shadow on the wall, that your mind wasn't playing tricks on you. Because I'm telling you, it'll take some hard and fast evidence to make Eric take this seriously."

"Well, what about the camera? I was taking pictures the whole time. . . ."

But Rohan was shaking his head again. "Yeah, we found it."

Rohan reached into his jacket and pulled out a stack of photographs. They were all the same—a mass of shadows and blurred images. Whatever that thing was in Simon's room, it wasn't easily captured on camera.

Daniel's hopes sank. It seemed that everything he'd done that night had been a waste of time.

"Rohan, I thought you were with Eric on all of this—obey the Rules and all. Accept what fate has in store for you, remember?"

Rohan looked at his friend. "I listened to you and I can tell you're telling the truth, Daniel. And to be honest, what you saw scares me.

"But maybe it was destiny that sent you to Noble's Green. So maybe it's our destiny to stop this—whatever it is—from ruining another kid's life." Rohan smiled a wicked smile. "Maybe it's our destiny to kick some butt."

Daniel laughed. Just when he thought he had his friend figured out, Rohan managed to surprise him.

"But we are going to need Eric." Rohan was serious again. "And, like I said—for that we need some *real* evidence."

Daniel tried to kick away the sheets in frustration, but as he did so, the stack of Johnny Noble comics began to slide off his lap and onto the floor. He reached over to stop them, but all he managed was to bump his cast against the bed rail. He winced as a jolt of pain went up his arm. This was going to take some getting used to.

"Here, let me get those," offered Rohan.

"Thanks," said Daniel, gesturing weakly with his broken wing. "Guess I'm not going to be much use for a while."

"Not so fast. If we're going to convince Eric before his birthday, then we are going to need you to do what you do best."

"Which is?"

"You're a detective, aren't you?" said Rohan, handing the books back to him. "Time to do some detecting."

Chapter Eleven
Written and Drawn by Herman Plunkett

The day after Daniel came home from the hospital, Gram went in. Gram's last chemo treatment had been especially strong, and she was now suffering from what his father described as "a sluggish immune system"—which meant that she was so weak that even a common cold could be dangerous. The doctors moved her to a special wing of the hospital where no visitors under fourteen were allowed. Until she got stronger, Daniel and Georgie wouldn't be able to visit her, but their mom went to the hospital every day and their father visited every evening.

Daniel missed her terribly. With Gram gone and his parents spending so much time up at the hospital, the old house seemed emptier, lonelier. His parents were obviously exhausted, though they tried not to show it. And seeing how tired they were, how much pressure the two of them were under, it was hard not to feel guilty about hurting himself. His parents thought that he had broken his arm in a stargazing accident—he told them that he had leaned too far out Simon's window and lost his balance. He felt bad about lying, but there was no way to tell them the truth without putting the Supers in danger—not that his parents would have believed him anyway. They had enough to worry about with Gram; they didn't need Daniel's crazy heroics adding to their stress.

So Daniel found himself with time on his hands—the doctors had told him to stay home from school for another week. In that time Georgie discovered a new favorite word, and that word was "NO." His brother waddled around the house wielding the word like a weapon.

"Georgie, time to eat."

"No."

"Georgie, time for bed."

"No."

"Georgie, let go of my hair."

"No."

Sometimes the only way to escape was to get out of the house, but since he wasn't allowed yet to go for walks (doctors' orders), he spent many an evening pacing the long wraparound porch out front. One evening he was just making his fifth turn when he saw Louisa biking up his driveway.

She waved and Daniel waved back. He was happy to have some company, but he couldn't help but remember what Rohan had said about her, and Daniel swore that if she ever "swooned" in front of him, he'd die. Plus, he still hadn't seen hide nor hair of Mollie, even though she lived right across the street.

But if he were to be perfectly honest with himself, there was something about Louisa that Daniel liked. Something very . . . well, *girl-like*.

"How are you feeling?" she asked as she sat down on the porch swing. She smoothed out her skirt and scooted over, leaving plenty of room for someone to join her—but not so much room that they'd be all that far apart. Mollie would've thrown her feet up and taken the whole swing.

Daniel decided to remain standing.

"I'm a lot better. The doctor says that I can go back to school on Monday, so I guess that's a good thing."

"I wrote out all the notes from science class for you," she said, reaching into her backpack. "We're studying genetics and the Human Genome Project this week."

She handed Daniel a sheaf of neatly written notes, complete with color-coded highlights. "Wow," said Daniel. "You didn't have to do that. I could've gotten them from Rohan when I got back."

"Well, I didn't want you to fall behind. And it's interesting stuff, mapping human DNA. Mr. Snyder said that it's like a big scientific puzzle, a mystery. And I know how much you like mysteries."

"Yeah, I do. Well, thanks, Louisa, these are great. Really, this is very . . . uh, sweet of you."

Louisa blushed prettily at the compliment. It was funny—whenever Mollie blushed, her face got all splotchy red, as if she were getting ready to break out in hives or something. Plus, the only times that Daniel had seen Mollie blush had been when she was angry—with her, compliments usually got you a punch in the arm.

And yet Daniel found himself glancing across the street at Mollie Lee's little yellow house.

Louisa folded her hands in her lap and began to gently swing herself on the porch swing.

"Simon's back at school," she said.

"Yeah. Rohan told me."

"You know, I was a little surprised when I heard that you'd been staying with him. When it all happened, I mean."

Daniel's breath caught in his throat. Their story had been that he, Rohan and Mollie had been camping out the night of Daniel's accident. They hadn't mentioned Simon at all.

"I wasn't . . . I mean, I was camping in the woods with Rohan and Mollie."

Louisa kept swinging on the swing. "Yeah, I know that's what you guys said, but I overheard you and Rohan at the hospital. It turned out that there *was* a soda machine just down the hallway from your room after all."

Now it was Daniel's turn to blush. She'd heard everything, or at least enough to guess at what had really gone on that night of Simon's birthday. If she told Eric now, before they'd had a chance to solve the mystery, they would all be in a load of trouble. He needed to convince Louisa to keep their secret. He needed to talk fast.

"Louisa . . . I . . . uh . . . oh . . ."

She looked at him and smiled. "Don't worry, Daniel. I'm not a snitch."

Embarrassed, Daniel breathed a sigh of relief. "I think I'll sit down now." He plopped down next to her and absently picked at his cast. "How much did you hear?"

"Not much. But enough to know that you guys are trying to stop it. Whatever *it* is."

"Well, we tried. But we failed. I mean, look at Simon, it's just awful."

"Is it? Is it really, Daniel?"

Daniel looked at Louisa then, blinking. They had stopped swinging.

"What do you mean? Of course it is! I mean, I don't even have any powers, but just the thought of losing them . . ."

"That's right, Daniel, you don't have any powers. You don't know what it's like to be different. To be a freak. Look, I know that Mollie and Eric and even Rose, they love having powers. They feel like it makes us special, unique. But what if I don't want to be special? What if I don't want to change the world? I just want to grow up, have friends, go to the movies and maybe even kiss a boy. . . ."

Gone were the coy looks, the smiles. Louisa was serious now, more serious than Daniel had ever seen her before.

"When you first joined us, Daniel, I was so happy. I *am* so

happy, just to be around you, because for the first time in my life I can forget what I am. I can just be a girl."

"But, Louisa, what I saw that night at Simon's . . . it wasn't right. What happened to him wasn't natural. Something is doing this to you and I know, deep in my gut, that it's wrong."

"Are you sure, Daniel? Are you really sure? Because what if you're wrong? What if the Rules are right and you guys are making a huge mistake that could be putting all of us in danger?"

Daniel had no answer. He hadn't actually seen that thing in Simon's room do anything to Simon. But he had felt it.

Louisa got up from the porch swing.

"Just be sure, Daniel. That's all I ask. You guys are my best friends and I'll always be on your side. But just be sure."

Louisa grabbed her backpack and slung it over one shoulder, smiling at Daniel again. "Anyway, I hope those notes are useful. Get better soon, okay?"

Then she turned and walked back to her bike. She gave a small wave and pedaled away, leaving Daniel alone with his thoughts, which were more confused than ever.

Back in his room, Daniel pored once more over the old issues of *Fantastic Futures, Starring Johnny Noble.* If there was a clue in there, he needed to find it now more than ever. Daniel was convinced that Louisa was wrong about what had happened to Simon, but she was right about one thing—he needed proof. It was irresponsible for him to act without it.

The pages were fragile, and Daniel had to be all the more

careful since he couldn't use his broken arm. Eventually he found a comfortable position at his desk, with the comics spread out before him and his cast propped up on a stack of books. The dull ache that had bothered him so much in the hospital was gone, only to be replaced by a constant tickle. Most of the time he could slide a pencil into the cast to scratch, but every now and then the tickle would creep just beyond the reach of even the pencil, and in those moments Daniel felt like smashing his head into a wall.

The one thing Daniel noticed upon rereading the stack of books was that this was not a complete set. There was a gap in the middle where the issues jumped from number seventy-six to seventy-nine. Two comics were missing from the collection.

Still, the rest of the books were obviously collector's items, and that was only part of their value. These stories were the closest thing that the Supers had to a history, and Rohan had shown a lot of faith in their friendship by trusting Daniel with them. And though he couldn't quite believe that the Supers were the legacy of some comic-book hero, Daniel wondered if there was another connection here that they were all overlooking.

He flipped open one of the books and studied the publishing credits on the first page. According to these, the comic came out in January 1946 . . . so long ago.

WRITTEN AND DRAWN BY HERMAN PLUNKETT

What a funny name, thought Daniel. He tried to picture Mr. Plunkett, a grown man sitting at his drawing table, cre-

ating stories out of the life of Jonathan Noble. What an imagination that guy must've had.

On a whim Daniel went online and typed in a name search. What he found was an archived newspaper article just a few months old, from the *Noble Herald,* and the headline read:

**Plunkett Philanthropies Donates
New University Library. Dedication
Ceremony Chaired by Resident
Herman Plunkett himself.**

Resident Herman Plunkett? Could it be the same man? That would mean he was still alive and living here in Noble's Green. Daniel decided to do a name-and-address search, and sure enough, there was an H. Plunkett on Cedar Lane. The man who created Johnny Noble had been living here in town all this time, and none of the Supers knew.

Cedar Lane was not far from Elm, and it took Daniel all of ten minutes to make the bike ride, even favoring his bad arm. If he made good time, he hoped he could be there and back before his dad returned with Georgie from day care. What was surprising was that Cedar turned out to be a private lane, with only a lone large house at the end of the street. Actually, "house" was an understatement. If there was a single mansion in Noble's Green, this was it. Tall pillars of white marble lined the broad entranceway of the immaculately kept front garden. A white old-fashioned arched roof peeked over the trees. Herman Plunkett had obviously done very well for himself.

As Daniel walked up the winding garden path to the front door, he played a little game with himself: he tried to guess what Herman Plunkett, the creator of Johnny Noble, might look like. Would he have a kindly face, bug-eye spectacles hanging from the bridge of his nose, maybe a big-bowled pipe like the one Sherlock Holmes smoked? Maybe he was still writing and drawing, and Daniel would find him hunched over his draftsman table, sketching away.

As he approached the pathway's end, Daniel noticed a well-dressed older gentleman standing a few feet away, reading the paper. The man wore an expensive suit and had a neat white beard. He smiled as Daniel approached.

"Excuse me," said Daniel. "I'm here to see Mr. Plunkett."

"Oh, I think you'll find him inside. Just ring the bell and tell his nurse you're here to see him."

"Oh, thanks," said Daniel.

"Not a problem, son," the man said with a smile, and went back to his paper. Daniel wondered what this man's job might be, standing out here all alone. Security maybe? He was a big guy, if a bit on the old side.

Daniel rang the front bell and, after a minute or so, a woman's plump face appeared at the door.

"Uh, hi. My name is Daniel Corrigan and I was wondering if I could speak to Mr. Plunkett? See, I'm a big fan of his work and I was hoping to get his autograph."

"Mr. Plunkett's work?" the fat nurse scoffed. "You're a fan of businessmen, are you?"

"Uh, no. His comic books. See, I have a bunch of comics that Mr. Plunkett drew a long time ago."

He opened his backpack and showed her the contents. With his arm in a sling, it was a struggle to do that much.

"Comic books, huh?" she asked, peering into the bag. "Well, I wouldn't know anything about that. Mr. Plunkett was a very well-regarded businessman in his day, but he's long retired now. And you really should try reading real books, you know. Those things will rot your brain."

Daniel sighed. This woman was a real pain. He looked over his shoulder to see if he might get some assistance from the well-dressed gentleman, but the man was gone.

"Hold on," said the nurse, looking him up and down. "I'll go and see if he's awake."

Awake? thought Daniel. *It's only four in the afternoon! Just how old is this guy?*

The nurse returned after a few long minutes. "Mr. Plunkett will see you. But you don't have any sweets on you, do you? Mr. Plunkett is on a strict diet and can't have any sweets."

"Um, no. No, I don't have any candy."

She glanced at his backpack. "You sure? You little boys are always carrying around chocolate bars or licorice drops. . . ."

Licorice drops? "Nothing, I promise! Can I please go see Mr. Plunkett now?"

"Fine, go on, go on. He's in the reading room, this way. But don't let him bribe you into sneaking him in any treats. He knows better!"

The reading room turned out to be a small annex off the main building, and through the large glass doors were rows and rows of books, newspapers and magazines. Several comfortable, overstuffed chairs dotted the room, each equipped with its own reading lamp. In the chair closest to the window sat a shriveled little man wearing an old sweater and bulky glasses. He was so small that his feet barely touched the floor, and his face was buried in an old paperback. Despite the thick glasses, he had the book pressed so close to his face that it almost touched his nose. On the book's cover was an illustration of a spaceman jet-packing toward an exploding rocket.

This had to be Herman Plunkett.

As Daniel opened the door, Plunkett's head popped up from behind his book, his beady eyes peering over the edge of his glasses.

"Eh? Who's there?"

The old man was surprisingly skittish—like a turtle ready to pop back into his shell.

"Excuse me, sir, but are you Herman Plunkett?"

"Who's asking?"

"My name is Daniel Corrigan. I think your nurse told you I was here."

"Eh? Oh, the boy with the comic books!"

"Yes, sir," said Daniel.

Plunkett slid down out of his chair and began cleaning a stack of newspapers off a nearby footstool. He shuffled the pile of papers onto a coffee table already weighted down with heaps of old encyclopedias and other reference books.

"Here you are, then," he said, patting the seat of the footstool.

Daniel let the reading-room door close behind him and sat down, his backpack held tightly in his good arm. Plunkett hopped back into his chair and folded his hands neatly in his lap.

"So, young man. Fancy yourself a comic-book aficionado, eh?"

"You bet," Daniel lied. "Actually, Mr. Plunkett, I'm really more interested in the classics. I'm a Golden Age fan."

"You don't say? Funny to find a boy your age who gives a darn about such things. Most youngsters these days are too interested in their video games, full of explosions and the like. No time for real stories."

Plunkett leaned in close and winked conspiratorially. "Say, you don't have any sweets in that little backpack of yours, do you? Maybe a licorice drop or two?"

"Uh, no, sir. I'm sorry."

"Shame. I sure could go for a licorice drop."

Daniel smiled uncomfortably at the old man and then looked around at the reading room that Herman Plunkett had constructed for himself. The stacks seemed to be made up almost entirely of old pulp novels and hardback adventure anthologies from the nineteenth and early twentieth centuries, all in mint condition. It was like walking into a library out of time. This Plunkett fellow was a man who had found his niche and stuck with it. One book in particular caught Daniel's eye—a brown leather-bound volume propped up alone on a side shelf. Although the gold lettering of the title was faded, Daniel could still make out the author—Sir Arthur Conan Doyle.

"Sherlock Holmes, *The Final Problem*," said Plunkett, noticing Daniel's interest. "You a Sherlockian, young man?"

"A what?" Daniel asked.

"A Sherlockian. A devotee of the world's greatest detective."

Daniel thought about it. He had never heard the term before, but he liked the sound of it.

"Yeah, I guess so. But I haven't read that one. It looks pretty old."

Plunkett hopped down from his chair and grabbed the volume off its shelf. For a little old man, he was surprisingly spry.

"*The Final Problem,* by Sir Arthur Conan Doyle, first published in 1893," said Plunkett, dusting off the spine. "This here is a later edition, but still valuable. One of the few books in my library *not* meant for reading. The death of Sherlock Holmes. Careful with it, now."

Plunkett handed the book to Daniel, who set it down gently on an empty table (it was too hard to hold with only one good arm). He carefully lifted the cover and reverently flipped through the first few pages. On the title page was an illustration of two men wrestling on a bridge, overlooking an ominous waterfall.

"It's a drawing of Holmes fighting his archenemy, Professor Moriarty, at Reichenbach Falls," Plunkett explained. "Their fighting pushes them both over the bridge, and they tumble over the falls to their shared doom. A grand death, very dramatic.

"Of course, Doyle brought him back eventually," Plunkett said with a smile. "No one stays dead for long in adventure stories."

Daniel studied the illustration in detail—the ominous scenery, the expressions of desperation on the faces of the two men. Daniel found it upsetting really, looking at the moment before the death of his hero. It took him a minute or so to find the artist's signature. There, hidden in the fine pencil work of the rushing waterfall, were the initials H.P.

"You drew this?" Daniel asked.

"I did! Back when I was a young freelancer. Back then I'd accept any hack job with a paycheck, but that one I'd have done for free. That was a labor of love."

Daniel closed the book and reached inside his backpack. He pulled out the bundle of plastic-bagged comics and set them in front of Mr. Plunkett.

"Did you also draw these?"

Plunkett squinted behind his thick glasses and held one

of the comics up to his nose. Daniel watched as his wrinkled face spread into a wide grin.

"Well, what do you know?" he said, thumbing through the other issues. "Hello there, Johnny!"

Plunkett settled back into his chair and, with great gentleness, began to turn the pages. He was drinking in every panel, every page.

"I haven't seen one of these in good condition in . . . well, I can't tell you, it's been so long. Where'd you get them?"

"A friend gave them to me. They were passed down in his family."

"Must be some friend! He know these babies are worth a pretty penny?"

"Yeah, but we're not interested in selling them."

"Good boy. Wow, will you look at how well the color held up? You know, I still have the pencils to some of these, but I haven't seen one printed in color in a long time. A long time."

Daniel had obviously gotten on Plunkett's good side with the revelation of a nearly full run of comic books written and drawn by Herman Plunkett. Right now, Plunkett was busy basking in the glow of his own fandom. Daniel didn't let the moment pass.

"So is it true that you wrote them all yourself? And you did the art?"

"It is. I was a young man when I did these, still chasing the dream of being a real artist. That was before I gave it all up and got a real job. I was always good at drawing *and* numbers, but there's a lot more money in numbers, as you can see." Plunkett gestured to the luxurious surroundings and Daniel nodded appreciatively. Daniel wasn't sure exactly what "numbers" he was referring to, but they obviously paid well.

"But this," said Plunkett, his attention back on the comics. "Well . . . this was my passion! I was working on *Fantastic Futures* back when it was just a science-fiction magazine. Then the world went crazy for superheroes and we started using Johnny as our lead story. Unfortunately, by the time we got rolling, the market had started to fill up. It's amazing that the book lasted as long as it did, really."

"How'd you come up with the character? I mean, was he based on anyone . . ." Daniel hesitated, unsure whether to warm up the old guy some more or plunge right in.

Plunkett gave Daniel a sideways look and sucked on his teeth. "I know what you're driving at. You think I stole Johnny from the folk stories, threw a mask on him and called him mine, don't you?"

Daniel opened his mouth to come up with an excuse, but nothing came out.

Unexpectedly, Plunkett just laughed. "Guilty as charged. But you gotta understand that it was just what folks did back then. Comics became a big business practically overnight, and there was a craziness to get in on the action. And being that I was from Noble's Green, I felt that I had some right to tell stories about him."

Daniel nodded. So it was true. Johnny Noble was just a stolen legend—the moneymaking scheme of a desperate young artist. The comics weren't the true-life accounts of a secret hero or the hidden clues to the mystery of a small group of super-children. Daniel's only lead had just hit a dead end.

Plunkett must have mistaken Daniel's obvious dejection for something else, because he reached up to the same shelf that the Sherlock Holmes book had rested on and brought down a dusty old folder.

"Tell you what, son. Since you came all this way, and since I'm impressed that anyone even remembers Johnny Noble in this day and age, I'm going to give you a present."

He used the sleeve of his sweater to dust off the portfolio and handed it to Daniel. Inside, neatly laminated, were original penciled pages from *Fantastic Futures, Starring Johnny Noble*. There was no ink or color and the dialogue was missing in places, but Plunkett's original pencil drawings were still breathtaking. His talent was undeniable, even back then. This was quite a treasure, and even though Daniel didn't find the answers he was looking for, this gift still touched him.

"Thank you," he said, and he meant it.

"Now if I see those popping up for sale on that Internet of yours, I'll be mighty disappointed!" said Plunkett, wagging his finger.

"They won't. I promise."

"All right, then, you better run along now. It's past my nap time, and old Nurse Hard-Butt out there gets mean when I miss my nap. But I'm glad you came by, my boy. You gave an old man a nice walk down memory lane. And remember, enjoy those sketches. Those are one-of-a-kinds!"

Back in his room, Daniel lay on his bed and stared at the ceiling, depressed. The trip to Plunkett's house had been a failure, and Daniel would have to report back to Rohan that all his detecting had turned up nothing more than some cool sketches. He had to admit it—he was stumped.

After a time the boredom finally got to Daniel and he went to his desk and opened Plunkett's portfolio. As he flipped through the pages of Johnny in action, he comforted himself with the knowledge that Eric, at least, would love this stuff. Here were the original drawings of Johnny lifting tanks, dodging bullets in midair and fighting for honesty and decency. Eric would treasure them, at least for the few weeks that he had left to be a kid. . . .

He was about a third of the way through the sketches when he saw it—the cover illustration of issue number seventy-seven. Heart pounding, hands shaking, he went to his backpack and searched through his stack of comics. Seventy-four, seventy-five, seventy-six . . .

Daniel went back and looked again at the cover of issue seventy-seven, the first of the missing magazines, laid out before him.

The cover featured a nighttime scene, a sleeping boy next to an open window. Outside the window, Johnny Noble was swooping down out of the sky. In the room, reaching for the boy's sleeping form, was a shadow. A shadow that Daniel had seen before. A shadow with a heart of fire.

The banner across the top of the page read:

INTRODUCING JOHNNY NOBLE'S TRUSTY NEW SIDEKICK AND HIS DI-ABOLICAL ARCHENEMY, BOTH IN THIS ONE FANTASTIC ISSUE! BUT WILL JOHNNY BE TOO LATE TO SAVE HIS NEW FRIEND FROM THE TERRI-BLE HANDS OF ... THE SHROUD?

The Shroud.

Breathless, Daniel sat back in his chair. Their enemy now had a name.

Chapter Twelve
Mollie's New Plan

That night Daniel could barely sleep. He kept replaying the day over and over in his head—the meeting with Herman Plunkett, the drawings of the Shroud. It was the same shadow that had taken Simon's powers away, the same shadow that had looked Daniel in the face, he was sure of it. Daniel suspected that he was the only boy in the history of Noble's Green who could remember seeing that shadow.

But what did it mean? Somehow Herman Plunkett had drawn the face of their enemy over half a century ago and today the only surviving pictures of the Shroud were Herman's own sketches. He'd said himself they were one of a kind. A crazy thought took root in Daniel's head—could

Herman Plunkett, that shriveled old man, in fact *be* the Shroud?

Looking back on it now, he found that things that once had seemed mundane took on sinister meanings. What had Plunkett really meant with all that stuff about the death of Sherlock Holmes? Was he trying to warn Daniel? To threaten him? In stories the villain often liked to toy with the hero, to play a game of cat and mouse before the final pounce. But that was in stories, and stories could not be trusted. In stories good always triumphed over evil, and like so many other children, Daniel had seen enough of the real world to know that wasn't always true.

The next morning he awoke groggy, and his bad arm stayed asleep. Once he started to move around, the blood came back to his arm and he winced as a thousand little needles pricked his skin. Because of the cast, he couldn't even massage the life back into it. All he could do was pound his fist into his pillow and say a bad word or two (which he did very, very quietly).

He finished his breakfast quickly and was ready to leave earlier than usual. His mother was already at the hospital visiting Gram, and his father was running late for work while trying to get Georgie ready for day care, so Daniel didn't linger. Consequently, he was early to the bus stop (a first). While he waited for the others to show up, he rehearsed what he might say to Mollie. If the shoe were on the other foot, she would probably start off with the silent treatment, but Daniel didn't have the patience for that. For once, he would do the talking and she would listen. He had risked his own life for her plan, and she hadn't even had the decency to come by and say thank you. He would need to cut to the chase, before she could accuse him of whatever crazy thing that, in *her* mind, *he* had done wrong. He would need to talk fast and loud, and he planned on gesturing to his broken arm a lot, for effect. After he had put Mollie in her place, then he would tell Rohan about Herman Plunkett and the Shroud. He might, *might,* let Mollie listen in.

As it happened, Mollie and Rohan arrived at the stop together. As soon as he saw them approaching, he made a big show of looking the other way—after all, he didn't want Mollie to think he had been waiting for her. He made sure that his broken arm was facing her as well, just for good measure.

"Hey, Daniel." It was Mollie's voice, which surprised him. He expected her to let Rohan do the talking, at first anyway.

Daniel tried to look surprised. "Oh, I didn't see you guys coming. . . ."

And that was as far as Daniel got, because when he turned around, he saw the one thing he never expected—Mollie was shamefaced.

She wasn't bawling—there were no heaving sobs or anything. But her face was red, and there were definitely the early signs of tears in her eyes and a slight quiver in her lip.

Daniel stole a glance at Rohan, who just gave one of his "What do *I* know?" shrugs.

"Uh," said Daniel. Not part of his planned speech.

"I'm sorry," whimpered Mollie. "Your arm, and Simon . . . it's all my fault and I am so, so sorry. I wasn't even brave enough to come and visit you. . . ."

"No, hey. It's okay! It's not your fault, really not at all," said Daniel. *Man, I'm a pushover,* he thought. *All it takes is a couple of tears.*

Crud, he thought, but he knew what he had to do next. Awkwardly, he put his one good arm around her.

"It's not your fault, Mollie, really it's not. And I think I know whose fault it is, because I've met him. Twice now."

Mollie wiped at her nose with the back of her hand. Daniel watched as she pulled herself together and the old Mollie came back to life. The Mollie that was itching for a fight with someone.

As for Rohan, he just smiled with pride. "Well, what do you know? That's our detective for you!"

On the bus ride to school, Daniel filled them in on his meeting with Herman Plunkett and his discovery of the Shroud. He had Plunkett's portfolio in his backpack, and both Mollie and Rohan practically shuddered when they saw the cover of issue seventy-seven. Daniel described again the shadow he had seen in Simon's bedroom, and no one could deny the eerie similarity to the image depicted in Plunkett's drawing.

Selling them on the idea that this little old man might in fact *be* the Shroud was another matter. And Daniel accepted that they had a right to be skeptical. After all, he wasn't sure what he believed himself. But Plunkett was the only lead they had, and Daniel couldn't shake the feeling that there was more to the old artist than he let on.

As usual, Mollie pointed out the obvious—if Plunkett was somehow in league with this Shroud, then it didn't make much sense to just hand his portfolio, the only real piece of evidence they had, over to Daniel. Rohan agreed that it was an odd move, but he was more concerned with why Plunkett would be terrorizing the children of Noble's Green. What could an old comic-book illustrator gain from it? To put it in detective terms—they had a suspect but no motive.

Whoever the Shroud was, *whatever* it was, it had stolen the powers of hundreds of children over the years, and it had taken their memories . . . memories of times spent with their friends, memories of doing remarkable things, of helping people. It was a kind of violence, what it did—of that Daniel was certain.

As they arrived at school, they were confronted with another problem—what to do about Eric. His birthday was just a few weeks away, and the plan had been to keep him in the dark until they had enough proof to convince him. But now, even with Plunkett's drawings in hand, they couldn't be sure how Eric would react. He believed in the legend of Johnny so strongly, with such conviction. To him the old stories and the comic books revealed a greater purpose to their powers, to their lives. The story of Johnny Noble promised a future— that they could all grow up to be heroes if they just tried hard enough. The bright, shining legacy of Johnny Noble was a way of life to Eric. How would he take the news that the truth might be something far darker—a thing shrouded in shadow?

As it happened, when they got off the bus Eric was waiting for them, leaning next to the school doors as groups of bustling students pushed and shoved their way past.

Eric folded his arms across his chest and looked Daniel in the eye. "Man, are you in trouble, Corrigan."

Daniel blanched. Even Rohan took a step backward, bumping right into Mollie.

"What are you talking about?" asked Daniel, his voice going an octave too high.

"Where's the Phillies cap I sent to the hospital? You know how hard it was for me to even touch that thing, much less buy one for you?"

Daniel breathed a sigh of relief. Of course Noble's Green didn't have a major-league baseball team, so Eric had chosen the nearby Pittsburgh Pirates as his. Their main rivals just happened to be Daniel's team, the Phillies.

"It's at home. Although I appreciate the gift, I didn't really want to wear it in front of you. Remind you how sucky the Pirates are doing this season and all. . . ."

Eric smiled. "Thoughtful of you. How's the arm feeling?"

"Itches. But otherwise it's okay."

"Must've been a heck of a tree that you fell out of. What were you doing climbing a tree at night anyway?"

"Well, uh," Daniel stuttered.

Mollie stepped in. " 'Cause I dared him to," she said. "So it's really all my fault."

"Well, I think he's got to share the blame for going along

with one of your crazy ideas. I thought you would know better by now, Daniel."

"Yeah, well. You know me, always showing off."

Eric smiled again, but Daniel thought he caught a flash of something else on his face. He told himself that he was just being paranoid, but for a split second he thought he saw Eric give him a look—a look that he hadn't seen before.

Whether Rohan saw it, too, Daniel didn't know, but it was Rohan who changed the subject.

"Have you spoken to Simon much?" he asked.

Now Eric was definitely troubled, and he made no effort to hide it. "Not at all. He barely seems to know who I am. He's a lot worse than any of the others. It's like, not only doesn't he remember the powers, he doesn't remember *us*. He knows who I am, but he doesn't remember that I'm his friend. Michael drifted away, but this is different. More . . . sudden. It's like he never even knew us."

No one said anything after that. Eric's birthday was next, but with the exception of Rose, they were all getting close. Losing your powers, and the memory of ever having powers, was bad enough, but losing the memories of your friends altogether was something else. This was a new kind of terror.

The ringing of the first bell kept them from dwelling on these maudlin thoughts, as the entirety of grades four through six scrambled to get to class on time.

Daniel had almost reached homeroom when Mollie grabbed him by his good arm (thankfully) and pulled him behind a stairwell.

"Hey, what are you doing? I'm going to be late!"

"We have to do something, Daniel!" Her eyes were wild with anger. Gone was the humbled Mollie of an hour ago—the old Mollie was back now and there was no one to save Daniel from her this time.

"Right now? Mollie, the bell just rang! Snyder will kill us!"

"You heard Eric! It's different now—it's worse! Eric is going to forget about us. Eventually we'll all forget."

Daniel tried to take his arm back but Mollie held on tight. He tried to look as if it weren't a struggle, but it was—he was caught.

"We don't know that for sure, Mollie. It might just be Simon."

"You don't believe that, Daniel. The Shroud saw you. He knows that we know about him, and this is his punishment! It's not fair!"

The halls were emptying out now, the last few stragglers running for their classrooms, hoping to make it before the second bell.

"We can talk about this later!"

"No!" Mollie's grip loosened and Daniel took his arm back, but he didn't bolt away. There was that something in Mollie's face, a determination in her eyes that kept him there just as surely as if she had pinned him to the floor. "You don't get it, do you? Eventually there won't be any of us *left* to remember—only you! You'll have all these memories, all these friendships, and we won't even know who you are. . . ."

The second bell rang, and then the hallway was quiet except for the sound of shutting doors. Mollie was quiet, too.

"All right," Daniel said. "What do you want me to do?"

"Tell your parents that we're doing homework together at my house. After school."

"That shouldn't be a problem. Why?"

"We're going to the other side of Mount Noble. We're going to the Old Quarry."

"The Old Quarry? But the Rules . . ."

"Well, we will just have to break the Rules. Again. We need answers, Daniel, and we are running out of time. Please, for Eric?"

Daniel swallowed hard and nodded.

Mollie nodded back, and Daniel watched as she turned and strode down the hall, her head held high. Mollie Lee was once again a girl on a mission, and strangely enough, Daniel was glad. It suited her.

Daniel followed her, but he didn't rush. He was already late; a few seconds more wouldn't matter. As he walked, he remembered that first day in the tree house and the reading of the Rules—

The North Face and the Old Quarry Are Off-Limits. Danger Waits for Us There.

Danger Waits for Us There. . . .

Today Daniel was very homesick for Philadelphia.

Chapter Thirteen
The Old Quarry

The trip to the Old Quarry took longer than either of them wanted. Daniel had expected them to fly there, but it turned out that he was a lot heavier than Louisa, and since Mollie wasn't super-strong like Eric, she didn't want to risk dropping him along the way. And since Daniel had no wish to be dropped, they decided to bike there instead. By the time they arrived, the sun had already started to set.

Daniel had only ever seen the south face of Mount Noble, and the difference was startling. On the south face, even at night you could still see the signs of civilization—hiking trails, the lights of far-off homes twinkling in the distance. But here, the wilds of nature dominated everything.

Tangled trees reached high into the sky, and the underbrush was thick and nearly impassable. Except for the quarry, there were no signs of humanity's touch at all. It was obvious to Daniel that for many, many years the north face had been off-limits to not just the Supers but everyone.

"It doesn't look like anyone's been here since the quarry closed," he said.

"No, I doubt that anyone has. The north face has always been an unlucky place. The quarry closed back in the fifties, after a bunch of bad stuff happened there. Some kind of accident or something. The Shawnee tribe had a strange name for this place—they called it Witch Fire Mountain."

Daniel stared at Mollie. "Who are you and what have you done with the real Mollie Lee?"

She gave him an indignant look. "What? Just because you're the detective doesn't mean that I don't know how to use the Internet, too. I did some research, that's all."

Daniel thought back to the first, and only, time that he had seen a picture of Jonathan Noble—not the comic-book character that he had inspired, but the real man.

"Mollie, I saw an old photograph of Jonathan Noble standing with a bunch of children, and there was something about a fire."

"The St. Alban's fire," she said. "Sure, it's in all the local history books. It's what made Jonathan Noble so famous. Before that he was just an ordinary fur trader."

Daniel remembered the look on those kids' faces—they were scared and tired. Even Noble himself was a mess, covered in dirt and soot. He hadn't looked much like a hero then: he'd looked like a man who had just been through something terrible.

"What happened?"

"St. Alban's was some kind of orphanage connected to a monastery up here. In the 1930s, the monastery burned down. Everyone was killed, except for the orphans themselves—Jonathan Noble was passing by when he saw the fire, and he risked his own life to save them. He rescued every single child."

Daniel looked around at the menacing trees and the deep black gorge of the quarry just a few feet away. "Let me guess," he said. "St. Alban's was never rebuilt and years later . . ."

"Yep. A mining company came in and dug a limestone quarry in the very same spot. The quarry suffered accident after accident, and eventually it was abandoned."

Daniel felt a small chill go up his spine at the thought of all that misery occurring in a single lonely place, on the dark side of this very mountain.

"And here we are," he said.

Mollie tossed him a backpack, then flipped on a flashlight and revealed a trail that wound off into the trees and disappeared into a giant pit, the size of a small valley, dug out of the side of the mountain itself.

"Here we are," she agreed, and with that she started down.

The path was dark and treacherous, carved out of the quarry walls. At one time it had been a winding road, wide enough to allow the workers' trucks and other machinery down to the quarry floor. But time and the elements had eroded much of the gravel and dirt away, and today the road was barely a footpath. At points it was hardly wide enough for a single person to squeeze by.

There were a few stumbles along the way, and at one point Daniel thought he saw something move along the path ahead of them. He and Mollie stayed frozen for about five minutes, shining their lights up ahead and listening to the sound of their own heartbeats. When nothing else happened, Mollie blamed Daniel's sighting on a coyote or bobcat crossing the path, which didn't make Daniel feel a whole lot better. Cautiously, they resumed their descent.

They reached the bottom without further incident, and Daniel was thankful when the sloping path leveled out onto firmer ground. These days the Old Quarry was hardly recognizable as a quarry at all. Over fifty years, nature had gone a long way toward reclaiming what humankind had taken away. The deep chasm still remained, but grass, shrubs and even a few small trees had taken root in the once-barren earth. The treasure here had been limestone, and exposed veins of the solid rock were still visible in the walls of the place, though they were hard to see in the fading daylight. There were plenty of corners and crannies down here that were hidden in blackness. Finding clues would be a task indeed.

The two intrepid explorers surveyed the area.

"This place looks creepy enough," said Mollie as she shone her flashlight in a broad circle around them.

"Well, there has to be a reason why it's forbidden. But more importantly," added Daniel as he eyed the desolate landscape, "forbidden by who?"

Mollie didn't answer, but the look on her face told Daniel that she was wondering the same thing. "C'mon," she said after a moment. "We didn't come here just to stand around worrying.

"Careful of sinkholes," she warned. "There are bound to be some deep ones around here that might have filled with water over the years. I'm a great flier but I'm kind of a lousy swimmer. I wouldn't be much help if you fell in."

Daniel followed Mollie deeper into the quarry, careful to shine his light on the ground in front of them. "So, what do you suppose we are looking for?" he asked.

"I dunno, Daniel. Clues, I guess. You're the detective!"

Clues, Daniel thought. *Right. In an overgrown quarry fifty years old. No problem.*

They had been at it for about ten minutes when something began to bother Daniel. The south end of the quarry, where they had come in, was wild and overgrown. Daniel was covered in scratches and cuts from all the thornbushes they had pushed through. But as they neared the north end, the underbrush cleared significantly. He found that he could walk without fear of stinging branches whipping him in the face. There weren't even any spiderwebs spanning the path ahead of them.

The path ahead of them . . .

"Mollie, stop," Daniel whispered. "Something's wrong

here. There aren't any thornbushes or hanging vines or anything else. It's a clear trail."

"So?"

"So who made the trail?"

Mollie's eyes grew wide as she understood Daniel's meaning, and for the first time since embarking on this fool's errand, Daniel allowed himself a little smile. Despite the danger, he couldn't deny that detective work was exciting stuff.

He got down on his hands and knees and started searching the ground, examining the weeds and bushes on either side of the trail.

"What are you doing?" Mollie asked.

"Shine your flashlight down here; I need more light."

It didn't take Daniel very long to find what he was looking for—a broken sticker-bush twig. He took the twig gently between his fingers and held it up to the light, pointing to the break.

"See? The wood's still green—that means the break is fresh. Someone's been through here recently."

Mollie looked at Daniel, impressed.

Daniel shrugged. "I read a lot."

Mollie smiled at this; then she shone her light along the path, first in the direction of where they had come from, and then where they were headed.

"Then how come there aren't any footprints?" she asked. "You can see ours clearly enough. You'd think that whoever broke that twig would've left some, too."

She was right. Whoever had been using this path was careless enough to clear the vegetation out of his way, but not enough to leave prints.

"I don't know," said Daniel, feeling uneasy. "Maybe we'll find the answer at the end of the trail."

They started again down the path, more cautiously this time, and walked for another few minutes before the path ended abruptly at a sinkhole, half filled with putrid water. The hole was about five feet across, too wide to step over and even too wide to jump. Shining their lights, they could see the trail continue on the other side and wind its way off into the blackness.

Mollie pointed her flashlight at the foul-smelling water and made a face. "Who builds a trail that leads straight into a scum-filled hole? It doesn't make any sense."

"You've got me. But we'll have to find a way around if we want to see where the rest of the path leads."

Daniel started testing out the ground on either side of the sinkhole, looking for safe passage. He could hear Mollie tapping her foot in frustration and impatience.

"Oh, for Pete's sake!" she said. Daniel almost let out a cry as she grabbed him around the waist.

"Mollie, what—"

"Just hold on."

She lifted the two of them off the ground, and they flew up in an arc over the watery hole. As they landed on the other side with a thump, a thought occurred to Daniel. "Of course!"

"What?" asked Mollie.

"You just showed me the one way someone could travel up and down this path and not leave any footprints. I was stupid not to think of it earlier—they can fly."

Mollie thought on this for a moment, but she didn't look convinced. "Well, we know it's not Eric, and we know it can't be Michael. So if there's another flier in Noble's Green, I guess it's about time I met them."

They walked the rest of the way down the path until they reached the far northern wall of the quarry. There, atop a small hill and under a short rock overhang, was the opening to a cave.

A quick examination showed that the entrance was sturdy, and wide enough for a full-grown person to walk through without having to duck. It looked as if the tunnel went back about thirty or so feet before stopping at a dead end. This time Daniel went first. Mollie, being a flier, hated small spaces, so Daniel suggested she remain near the entrance.

Daniel crept along the dark passageway as silently as he could. Unfortunately, the tunnel echoed with every disturbed pebble. Gritting his teeth against the sound of his own steps, Daniel reached the end. So far the cave had been unremarkable, a natural leftover from the days when men bored into this earth for stone, but here at the end was something else.

The tunnel didn't stop on its own; rather, someone had stopped it. A large disk of solid rock blocked the pathway, like a manhole cover tilted on its side. Two great iron handles were bolted into its face, and the walls around it were scuffed and chipped, a clear indication that this thing had been moved repeatedly. But it would take someone with strength far beyond that of the strongest man to move it.

Daniel had just begun to search the cave wall for some kind of hidden lever when he caught sight of his own breath in the glow of his flashlight. He realized then that he had instinctively pulled his jacket closer. There was a new chill in the air.

Daniel turned his head and saw Mollie standing in the cave entrance, hugging her arms to her sides to keep warm. Just over her shoulder, silhouetted in the twilight, a black shape floated. A shape darker than the surrounding shadow, a shape that Daniel now had a name for. . . .

The Shroud! His mind screamed the name, but his voice was caught in his throat, choked off by his fear. For an instant he couldn't move, he was trapped in the memory of that night at Simon's window, the terror of falling. . . .

Mollie called to him, "Hey, did you find anything? Hurry up, it's getting freezing out here."

Daniel swallowed his fear and found his voice as the Shroud reached for Mollie. "Behind you!"

Until that moment, Daniel hadn't known just how fast Mollie was. Not really. He had witnessed her speed in races with Eric, but what he saw before was nothing compared to what he saw now. Or more accurately, what he didn't see—it all happened too fast. The Shroud reached out a ragged hand of shadow that barely brushed Mollie's shoulder, and instantly she was gone. She must have felt the cold of that touch because Mollie turned into a flash—a girl-shaped blur that was at the cave entrance one second and standing next to Daniel, grabbing at his sleeve, the next.

"OhmygoshDanielisthathim?" Mollie's powers were so revved up that she was even speaking at super-speed. Daniel could barely make out her words.

"*The north face is forbidden. Danger waits there.*" The Shroud's voice echoed through the cave like the rustle of dead leaves and the snapping of dry twigs . . . or bones. The shape that rose up to prevent their escape was larger than Daniel remembered, its billowing black cloak snuffing out the light of their flashlights, its bulk blocking their path. Wisps of darkness seemed to undulate around its body, and its green heart of fire pulsed in slow rhythm.

Daniel had the dread suspicion that he and Mollie had just discovered the author of the Rules. The Rules weren't meant to protect the children; they were meant to protect this thing, to keep its home safe. And the two of them had just been caught trespassing.

Mollie grabbed hold of Daniel's cast. He put his good hand on hers to calm her, but he realized she wasn't looking for reassurance; she was gently pulling him away. She was leading him slowly, slowly, toward the entrance of the cave, toward the Shroud.

"What are you doing?" he whispered.

"We're cornered. Trapped. We need to get outside. Whatever you do, don't hesitate. Follow me as fast as you can, then just keep running."

Daniel stared at the shadow blocking their escape and wondered how they could possibly make it past. It nearly filled the cave. And it was getting closer.

"I just hope it's solid," she said.

"What? Why?"

"So that I can do *this*!" Mollie let go of Daniel's arm and flew, straight as an arrow, toward the Shroud. She slammed like a bullet into the chest of the thing. As it turned out, the Shroud was quite solid, because Daniel heard it gasp as the wind was knocked out of it. Its great swelling blackness crumpled around little Mollie Lee as the two of them tumbled out of the cave's mouth and out of view.

Despite Mollie's instructions, Daniel didn't move right away. He was in shock. One minute the Shroud was blocking their path, and the next Mollie was flying into the creature and disappearing down the hill. . . .

Mollie!

Daniel snapped to his senses and ran for the mouth of the cave. When he reached the outside, he saw Mollie lying some twenty feet down the hill. She had landed in a bunch of tall grass, and though she was moving, she looked pretty dazed.

Unfortunately, the Shroud was still conscious as well. It had landed only a few feet from Mollie and was standing, or, more accurately, floating upright.

Daniel glanced to his left and saw the path clear ahead of him. The way out of the quarry was unguarded, and Daniel had plenty of time now to make his escape—just as Mollie had wanted. But that wasn't what Daniel wanted. There was no way that he was going to leave her here with that thing. It had stolen the powers and memories of countless children just for the crime of turning thirteen. Who knew what it might do to Mollie, now that she had invaded its lair. But what could an ordinary boy with a broken arm do against such a monster?

"Hey! Hey, Ugly! Up here!"

It was not one of Daniel's best plans. But in the heat of the moment, sometimes there isn't time for thinking. Sometimes you just have to act.

The Shroud turned its head toward Daniel and seemed to be studying him, judging whether he was enough of a threat to warrant immediate attention. Daniel needed to get it away from Mollie, so he decided to stack the odds in his favor with some good old-fashioned trash-talking.

"You know, I'm not one of your Supers, so your stupid little Rules don't apply to me. I think I'll come around here all I want. Matter of fact, I might bring some other people, too, like the local sheriff, maybe even the Department of Homeland Security. . . ."

It was enough. The Shroud hissed and reared back its faceless head before slinking across the ground and up the hill toward Daniel.

Unfortunately, this was as far as Daniel's plan went. In

just a moment, the Shroud would have him, and Daniel had no weapons other than his flashlight. Remembering the encounter at Simon's window, Daniel decided to try a desperate trick. He waited until the Shroud was just feet from him, then he flicked on his flashlight full in its eyes, or at least where its eyes would be if it had them. Even this close up, Daniel could make out no more detail than before. It was as if someone had cut away a shroud of shadow and given it form, with only that sickly green heart to disturb the blackness.

As before, the flash of light seemed to make it hesitate. It slowed its attack and even pulled back slightly. But Daniel's flashlight was still only a flashlight. On its second advance it dove to the right quickly, avoiding the direct glare of the beam. In one fluid move, the Shroud batted the light from Daniel's hands, and all he could do was watch as it clattered down the rocky slope. Daniel felt his breath catch in his chest as he watched long fingers of shadow creep out from the thing's hands, which were flexing and clawing eagerly at its side.

But to Daniel's surprise, it didn't turn those hands on him. Instead it stayed still, and Daniel could feel the monster's stare even if he couldn't see its eyes.

"Such a smart boy. So smart and so brave for one so weak. So soft, and so . . . breakable."

The Shroud gestured to Daniel's broken arm. Again, its raspy voice grated along his nerves, making the hairs stand up on the back of his neck. Something in its pitch, its timbre, made every impulse in him scream, "Run!" But he held his ground. If he tried to flee, he had no doubt that it would overtake him anyway.

"You're . . . you're right. I'm not one of them." Daniel's own voice had lost its earlier bluster. Now he couldn't disguise the terror he was feeling.

"What are you, then?"

"I'm . . . I'm just a boy."

"Ah, now there you are wrong."

Daniel felt then a gust of wind, and the next thing he knew, he'd been knocked off his feet and yanked up into the air. Something had a hold of him, and that something was Mollie.

"We're leaving!" she yelled. "Hold on tight!"

He wrapped his good arm around her waist and watched as the ground disappeared below them. Mollie's face was red and the veins in her temple bulged with the effort, but pure adrenaline was giving her the strength she needed now. For Daniel's part, he looked down at the disappearing ground and willed himself to think light thoughts.

They had broken above the tree line and Mollie was just making the turn toward Noble's Green when Daniel saw the creature rising up through the trees. The Shroud was giving chase, and it was gaining. Ordinarily, Daniel wouldn't have doubted that Mollie could outfly it, but with his extra weight, they were losing ground.

Mollie felt it, too. Without warning, she changed direction and flew up—straight up.

"Where are you going?" Daniel shouted, his voice barely carrying over the wind.

"An old trick of Michael's! Hang on!" And with that she flew faster, aiming for a bank of low clouds that had settled around the peak of Mount Noble.

The Shroud was only a few feet behind them when they entered the clouds. The night sky disappeared in the black mist, and Daniel felt the little pellets of rain sting his face as the air turned cold.

They were twisting, turning, changing direction, but by now Daniel was too disoriented to know if it was on purpose or if Mollie was simply lost as well. They were flying blind, and Daniel even wondered if she knew which way was up.

The Shroud appeared out of nowhere. One second they were alone in the dense mist, the next the creature was blocking their path. Luckily, it seemed as startled as they were, and it hesitated for half a second. Half a second was all Mollie needed to drop below its reach and disappear once more into the murky vapor.

Daniel felt another lurching change of direction, and when they broke the cloud cover, they found themselves high in the sky, looking down at the storm bank. The cold wind up here was bitter and thin, and Daniel's ears and fingers began to sting with frost.

"There!" Mollie shouted. "Found one!"

"Huh?" Daniel managed between chattering teeth.

"A current!" Mollie said with a smile. "Now we let the wind fly for us!"

Then they were diving, barreling through the sky and clouds, past trees and mountain.

Daniel managed to squint behind them and see that they had escaped the Shroud with Mollie's desperate dive. Once more they flew alone—alone while hurtling at a fantastic speed toward the lights, and hard ground, of Noble's Green.

As they flew faster still toward the ground, Daniel noticed that Mollie was no longer smiling.

"Uh-oh, too fast," she muttered. He couldn't really hear her in the roar of the wind, but he could read her lips well enough, because it was what he was also thinking as the ground rushed up to meet them.

Uh-oh.

Chapter Fourteen
Journey Home

Agood soak wasn't too much of a price to pay for surviving a high-speed chase with a shadowy, memory-stealing monster. Daniel was so sure of this that he repeated it to himself over and over again as he sloshed his way along the long road home to Elm Lane.

Their landing had been rough, to say the least. It was only due to Mollie's extraordinary flying that they weren't impaled on a bunch of trees or flattened against a roof. As it was, she had managed to steer their fall into Tangle Creek, skidding along the water's surface to slow their momentum, until the only damage done was a record-setting splash.

All that was left was the walk home. Mollie was so exhausted that she could barely stand, much less fly. So Daniel helped her along, his good arm around her waist. The fact that she accepted his help at all was proof of just how worn-out she was.

With every step, dirty creek water squirted out of Daniel's sneakers. He looked down at his dripping cast and grimaced. Even if Daniel managed to make it home and into his bedroom without being noticed, even if he managed to hide his soggy clothes, the cast would be a dead giveaway. The mucky water of Tangle Creek had given the plaster a greenish tinge that would be impossible to hide. No matter what, his bad arm would rat him out.

It took a while, but eventually his one-foot-in-front-of-the-other strategy paid off and they made it back to Elm Lane, although it was a good two hours past his curfew. Daniel wasn't surprised to find his parents waiting for him.

Daniel had expected Mollie to go straight home, as her parents were probably worried as well, but instead she walked with him all the way to his front porch, where he found his father pacing back and forth.

"Daniel," his father said. Daniel decided that a preemptive strategy would work best—throw himself at his father's feet and hope for mercy.

"Dad, I'm sorry I'm so late. But Mollie and I were taking a walk after dinner, and we lost track of where we were."

His father glanced at the children's damp clothing, their streaked, muddy faces. "A walk? Which lake were you walking in, exactly?"

"Well, like I said, we got a little lost. . . ."

"Never mind about that now. Mollie, you'd better run along home, your parents are worried sick." Something in his dad's tone bothered Daniel. He seemed distracted . . . and much, much too calm. He should've been furious with him.

At that moment Daniel's mother appeared at the door. Her eyes were bloodshot and her face puffy—she had been crying.

"Mom," Daniel said. "I'm all right, I'm okay."

"Oh, honey," she said, and then went back into the house. Daniel could hear her sobbing as she went up the stairs.

Bewildered, he looked back to his father, who put a hand on Daniel's shoulder. "Daniel, we need to talk. It's about Gram."

"What?" Daniel demanded. "What about her?" His earlier fear was gone, replaced by something fiercer. He didn't even notice that he was practically shouting at his own father.

"Daniel . . . she's gone."

Daniel didn't hear what his father said after that. His world suddenly got very small, and the pounding of his own heart made him deaf to anything else. He turned back to Mollie—had she heard the same thing? Perhaps Daniel was imagining all of this and Mollie could simply punch him in the arm and tell him to snap out of it.

But Mollie wasn't there. She wasn't anywhere.

One minute she was right behind him, and then the next, she was gone.

Chapter Fifteen
Flowers and Casseroles

Daniel's shirt collar was overly starched and scratched against his neck, and his shoes were too tight, forcing him to keep flexing his toes so that they wouldn't fall asleep. He had already gotten rid of that awful tie—a blue and black one that he'd had to wear to church back in Philadelphia—and he wondered if it would be rude to take off his shoes as well and just walk around in his socks. There was a hole in one of them, over his right pinky toe, but that shouldn't matter. A boy should be able to walk around his own house with holes in his socks.

What prevented him from doing so was that his house was full of strangers—Daniel refused to call them *guests*.

Guests were people you invited to a party or some other kind of joyful event, but these people all came together because something awful had happened. And now they were all in Daniel's house, eating and drinking together for some reason that Daniel couldn't begin to understand.

The funeral had been earlier in the day. Daniel's parents drove them out to the small church that Gram used to go to, before she got sick. There was a reverend who said some nice things about Gram, and then he said a whole lot more about God and heaven and stuff. Daniel thought he spent far too much time on God, and wished he'd talked a little more about Gram, but he seemed kind enough and he shook Daniel's hand when it was over and told him to be brave.

Then they drove out to the cemetery and some more people said some more nice things. Daniel's mother started to say something, but she got too upset to talk, so his father stepped in and put his arms around her. Daniel heard her saying, "My mom's gone," over and over, and this struck Daniel as strange for some reason. Gram was just Gram—he didn't think of her as someone's mom. In the same way, Daniel's mother was just Daniel's mother—he didn't think about her being someone's daughter.

When they came home, everyone came with them.

They all brought over food—sandwiches, potato salad, cakes and pies and too many casseroles to count—which Daniel figured was supposed to be a nice gesture. But he wondered what they would do with all that stuff since there was no way one family could ever eat so much. It seemed like an awfully big waste.

So with a house full of strangers bearing food, Daniel found himself sitting on the back porch with Georgie, tugging at his over-starched collar. Georgie was lucky, Daniel thought. Their parents had changed him out of his nice clothes the minute they got home. They were probably afraid that he would get them all dirty, which in fact he would have. He was sitting in the dirt right now, putting one of his favorite balls into the back of a toy truck, dumping it and then starting all over again. He had been at it for twenty minutes and seemed nowhere close to quitting.

When the back door opened, Daniel turned around, expecting to see another of the adults offering their condolences and some more food, but he was surprised to find a strange girl he didn't recognize standing behind the screen. She was wearing a dark dress with a lacy collar and white stockings. Her hair was done up in braids.

"Are you one of my cousins?" Daniel asked.

"Are you a *moron*?" the girl snapped back.

Daniel did a double take.

"M-Mollie?"

Mollie came out onto the porch and let the door clang shut behind her. She sat down next to Daniel on the steps and smoothed out her skirt while tugging at her stockings.

"I didn't recognize you. In that dress, and your hair . . ."

"Not. Another. Word."

Daniel said nothing, but he couldn't resist a smile. It was the first time he'd smiled in days.

"My mom and dad are inside talking with your parents. They brought over a casserole and told me to see if you wanted anything to eat."

Daniel rolled his eyes. "No thanks."

"Rohan's here, but some woman has him cornered and won't stop pinching his cheeks."

"That would be my mom's great-aunt Flora. She never had any kids of her own and, well . . . I got the Flora treatment earlier." Daniel rubbed his left cheek. It was still sore.

"So. Are you okay?"

"I'm okay," answered Daniel. Then the two of them sat together for a while and watched Georgie and his dump truck.

Eventually Rohan joined them. He was wearing a smart little bow tie and a dark suit that was too big in the sleeves.

"That woman must be stopped," he said, rubbing the feeling back into his cheek. "She's just lucky I don't have super-strength."

The three of them sat on the porch and chatted about nothing for a while. Daniel had hoped that people would get tired and go home early, but instead the noise from inside the house just got louder. More people were showing up every minute, and Daniel was glad that they hadn't yet spilled out to the backyard.

Eventually the conversation turned to the night at the

quarry. Daniel couldn't believe that it had happened only three nights ago—to him it seemed like something out of another life entirely. Someone else's life.

Mollie had already told Rohan about the Shroud and the tunnel with the solid-rock door, but now was an opportunity to fill him in on the details. Mollie went through their whole adventure together, play by play, while Daniel sat silently, picking at the paint peelings on the porch steps. Occasionally Mollie would ask Daniel if she was getting some little detail right, and he would nod or offer a clarification. But all this was a story Daniel had no desire to be a part of again, even if it was just in its retelling. His mind was on Gram. He'd meant to spend more time with her, but there always seemed to be something else that needed doing. His friends, his superpowered friends, had needed him while his gram got sicker and sicker. Apparently Daniel had chosen his priorities, and he'd chosen wrong.

"Well," said Rohan after Mollie was finished. "I think that settles it. We need to tell Eric."

Mollie said nothing but looked at Daniel instead.

"What?" he said. "You guys can do whatever you want."

"Yeah," said Mollie. "I know that. But I want to know what you think."

"What I think is that I don't want to think about this anymore."

"Daniel's right," said Rohan. "This isn't the time to make decisions."

"No, you don't understand," said Daniel, turning to look

at them. "I mean I don't want to think about this ever again. This was never my business to begin with. I can't fly. I can't see mountains on the moon, and when I wake up on my thirteenth birthday, I will be the same as I was the day before — ordinary."

"Daniel," began Rohan, but Daniel didn't let him finish.

Daniel stood and scooped Georgie into his arms. Georgie began to whine and reach for his toy truck, but Daniel ignored him. He carried him back up the steps and into the house. In the doorway he paused and looked back once more at his friends.

"I'm sorry," he said. "But I'm just a plain, useless kid. I can't save anybody."

Then he shut the door and let the noise of the party swallow him up.

Inside, Daniel walked Georgie past crowd after crowd of well-wishers offering sympathetic pats on the head. Georgie loved the extra attention, and since he was too young to understand about Gram's death, Daniel felt as if he should be carrying little Georgie's grief around with his own. It would have been the big-brotherly thing to do, but he just didn't have room for it. Daniel's own hurt was too big.

He found his mother in the dining room. She was sobbing again, and a few kindly-looking old ladies were rubbing her back and handing her tissues.

"The whole time I just kept wishing there was something I could do," he heard her say. "I just felt so damn helpless."

Daniel's mother never cursed. Not even that mostly harmless word. He turned and left the dining room without letting her know he had been there.

He was on his way back to the kitchen when he saw the older man—tall and strong-looking, standing off in one corner alone. His black suit looked expensive, not like Daniel's father's rumpled, all-purpose gray one that he was wearing today.

The man looked at Daniel and smiled. There was something familiar about him—he recognized the white-bearded grin that had greeted him outside Plunkett's mansion.

"Hey, Daniel," came a sudden voice from behind him.

Daniel turned and saw Eric coming over to him. Eric wasn't dressed up like everyone else, and for some reason that pleased Daniel immensely.

"Hey, Eric, I . . ." Daniel's words were lost somewhere in his throat.

Eric seemed to understand. He just nodded and put his hand on Daniel's shoulder. When he let go, Daniel looked back to where the well-dressed man had been standing, but he'd disappeared. Plunkett's man, whoever he was, was gone.

Eric picked up Georgie and bounced him in the air, to Georgie's squealing delight. "How're you holding up with all this?" Eric asked, gesturing to the crowds and buffet tables that had invaded Daniel's home.

"I'm all right, I guess. I wish this were a little less of a party."

"Yeah, I guess grown-ups deal with death by drinking and

eating. My mom did a lot of drinking, I mean a *lot* of drinking, when my dad died."

Daniel looked at him in shock. He'd gathered from previous conversations that Eric's dad wasn't around anymore, but he'd assumed that Eric's parents were divorced. It had never occurred to him that Eric's father might not even be alive.

"Eric, I didn't know about your dad. . . . I'm sorry."

"Yeah, well, it was a long time ago. I was only five when he got sick. Mom tried over the years to get me a new dad. Several. But it turns out her taste in men has gotten worse and worse."

"So . . . Bob?" asked Daniel, remembering the blue Chevy parked outside his home.

Eric shrugged. "Another deadbeat. My mom threw him out again last week, but he'll just come crawling back sooner or later."

"How do you do it, Eric?"

"Do what?"

"How do you deal with . . . so much? I mean, I just lost Gram and I am so angry right now that I . . ." Daniel stopped. Again, he couldn't go on.

Luckily, he didn't have to. "Look, it's not like I never get angry," said Eric. "Believe me, I do. Sometimes I get so angry I scare myself.

"But, you know, that's what being a hero is all about, right? Overcoming your fears and failures to help other people, like Johnny Noble did." Eric smiled. "I know you cringe when I talk like that but it's true."

"I don't cringe," Daniel protested.

"Yes you do. So does Mollie. You guys are afraid that one day I'll show up in a cape and tights and that will be it! But the whole idea of being a superhero is not about any of that. It's about being a better person. And Johnny is an example that shows me what it is to be brave. And I'm not even talking about having powers or being a Super or anything. I'm just talking about being the best person that you can be, and that means not giving in to anger, or fear. It's what keeps me going, even though there are people like Clay Cudgens out there in the world. And people like Bob. All I've got is the hope that I will wake up on my thirteenth birthday the same as I was the day before. I can only do my best and believe that one day I'll be able to do more."

"The First Rule — Use Your Powers to Help. Never Hurt," said Daniel.

"You bet your butt," said Eric with a smile.

"Ball!" shouted Georgie, pointing to the front yard.

"Sorry, buddy," answered Eric. "Maybe later."

Eric handed Georgie back over to Daniel and looked around. "Are Rohan and Mollie here? I've been trying to talk to them for days, but it's like I'm getting the cold shoulder."

"Last I saw them, they were out back."

"Oh. And why aren't you out there with them?"

Daniel almost told him everything, right there and then.

Plunkett, the Shroud, the truth about Johnny Noble—everything. But then he thought about what Eric had said, and how his belief in Johnny kept him going every day despite all his troubles, and he just couldn't do it. He couldn't be the one to shatter all of Eric's dreams. Someone would probably have to before this was all over, but it wouldn't be Daniel.

"Why don't you go on out there," Daniel said. "I've got some stuff to do in here. They'll be glad to see you. I'm sure you all have a lot to talk about."

Eric gave Daniel a skeptical look, but he let it slide. "Okay," he said. "I'll see you later?"

"Sure," answered Daniel, but in truth he wasn't sure. He'd just made up his mind about something. A few minutes ago he'd been ready to throw it all in, to let the Supers—his friends—struggle on their own. Thinking back on what he'd said to Mollie and Rohan, he grew ashamed.

After everything Eric had been through over the years, he still hadn't given up. With his power he could have easily gone down the same path Clay had taken. He could've become a bully, or worse, and there would've been no one to stop him. But Eric decided to use his powers to help people instead, without so much as a thanks.

Use Your Powers to Help.

Daniel watched as Eric headed for the back door, grabbing a handful of white cake on his way out. Alone, Daniel looked around for the well-dressed stranger but couldn't find him again. He'd disappeared among all the flowers that were piling up in the living room. Any space that wasn't already occupied by food was now claimed by a bouquet or potted plant.

Across the crowded room he saw that Louisa and Rose had arrived, and the two of them intercepted Eric on his way out back. Daniel couldn't hear what they were saying, but he saw Eric point to him, and then Louisa gave Daniel a small, sad smile. Daniel smiled back and made his way to greet the two sisters. Today he would suffer through the food and the consoling pats on the back and the awkward small talk, because tomorrow he had a big day ahead of him. Tomorrow he was going back to Plunkett's mansion. For his friend Eric, for all of them, he would face the Shroud once and for all.

Alone.

Chapter Sixteen
Plunkett's Story

"Eh? Well, if it isn't the little fanboy. What can I do for you today, Mr. Corrigan?"

"I'm sorry, Mr. Plunkett," said his fat nurse, scurrying after Daniel. "The little creature just pushed past me and ran!"

Daniel was standing inside the doorway to Plunkett's library. The little man was in his usual spot, sunk into his overstuffed chair like a turtle in his shell.

"That's quite all right, Angie. I've been expecting another visit from Daniel, haven't I?"

Daniel reached for his backpack and undid the zipper. Plunkett made no move, but he watched Daniel with a wary fascination.

Daniel plopped the comics from the tree house down in front of Plunkett. Then he tossed the old man's drawings down next to them.

"You can go now, Angie," said Plunkett, his eyes only glancing at the bundle of sketches in front of him. "Thank you."

Angie shot Daniel one last dirty look and then turned on her heels and walked away.

"I get it, Plunkett," Daniel said after she'd gone. "And I'm here to tell you that it's over. I don't want to play your silly game anymore."

Plunkett was quiet for a moment; then he looked out into the open hallway behind Daniel. "Close the door," he murmured.

The door was mostly glass, so anyone outside could see everything that was going on in the reading room, but Daniel still felt uneasy about closing off his only escape. Still, he did as he was told. After all, he was here to put a stop to all the attacks.

"So, we're dropping pretenses, are we?" the old man sighed. "You stop pretending to be a wide-eyed comics fan and I stop pretending to be a doddering old fool? Good. That will make all this much easier."

Plunkett pulled himself down from his chair with a resigned groan. "Though my mind may not have gone soft, I'm afraid that my body has. I'll tell you, kid, it's a drag getting old."

He shuffled over to a tea cart that had been set up near

the reading room's bay window. "Care for a cup?" he asked. Daniel said nothing.

Plunkett winced in pain as his bones creaked, and his hand shook slightly as he struggled to pour the tea without spilling it. He seemed so infirm, so fragile, that Daniel found himself wondering if he wasn't crazy for being here. Daniel had seen the creature that was preying upon the children of Noble's Green; he'd felt its dark power face to face, its strength. This tiny man was barely strong enough to pour a cup of tea. But somehow Plunkett knew about the Shroud; he'd drawn it years before Daniel or any of his friends had even been born. And the most convincing evidence that the old man was involved in all of this was the fact that Daniel felt it in his gut. Maybe it was something in Plunkett's manner that made him suspicious, maybe it was simple kid's intuition, but Daniel was sure that the old man was more than he seemed, and Daniel was sick of the lies.

"I saw your man at my house after the funeral yesterday. I recognized him from the last time I was here."

Plunkett cocked his head. "My man?"

"The one who wears the nice suits. The guy with the beard. I assume that he's your bodyguard or whatever. And you sent him to my house to spy on me and my friends."

Plunkett surprised Daniel by not responding immediately. The man normally seemed tickled with his little game playing, but now he appeared genuinely confused. And perhaps a little anxious. When he spoke next, he seemed to be only half talking to Daniel, more interested in some inner argument he was having with himself.

"Well, I'm sure I don't know what you're talking about. There is no such gentleman in my employ. It's true that I have eyes and ears throughout Noble's Green, but none of them match that description."

Plunkett sniffed and rubbed his hands together. The matter was apparently settled. He went on, "I was sorry to hear about your grandmother, though. Believe me when I say that she was a special person."

"You knew my gram?" Daniel asked, cautious.

"I've lived here a long time. I know a lot of people. It's a strange thing to outlive everyone you know. . . ." Plunkett's shoulders slumped and he got a faraway look in his rheumy eyes as he sipped at his tea. For a moment, Daniel actually felt sorry for the old villain. But then he silently reminded himself who he was really dealing with and what the man had done.

Plunkett recovered. "Now then," he said, wiping his eyes on his sweater sleeve. "On to business—you've found him, have you?"

Plunkett didn't wait for Daniel's answer; instead he clapped his hands together as if he'd just won a prize. "I wasn't sure my clue would work, but I figured that if you were a detective worth your salt, you'd eventually figure it out. I've been holding on to those drawings for many, many years, and I was loath to part with them. But it was the best way to make sure you were ready."

"Ready for what?" asked Daniel, struggling to sound less confused than he really was.

"Why, to battle the Shroud, my boy!"

"I don't want to fight you," said Daniel, backing up a step. "I came here to ask you . . . to reason with you. Please leave my friends alone."

"Fight me? Fight *me*? Why, what are you . . . oh, I see. My, oh my. You think *I'm* the Shroud?"

Daniel said nothing, but his face told all.

Without warning, Plunkett began to laugh. The old man laughed so hard that he ended up bent over in a coughing fit. "Well, that's what I get for trying to play it sly, eh? I've got you thinking that I'm the Shroud!

"My boy, while I can certainly understand how comforting it would be for you and your super-friends to find out that your archnemesis was really just an infirm old geezer, I'm afraid you've got it wrong. I'm no monster. I'm no master criminal. I'm just plain old Herman Plunkett—old man and fool."

He reached for a second cup from the tea cart. "Are you sure you won't change your mind about that tea?"

Daniel again refused, but he did allow himself to sit on the old leather footstool, lest he fall over. His mind was spinning, trying desperately to process this revelation. This was just another one of Plunkett's lies. It had to be.

"Why should I believe you?" asked Daniel.

Plunkett smiled. "Why not? Because it's easier to believe

that I'm really a menacing creature that preys on the innocent children of Noble's Green, stealing their powers away in the night?"

"B-b-ut," said Daniel, "if you're not the Shroud, then how do you know about . . . my friends?"

"I said I wasn't the Shroud, Daniel. I never said I was stupid."

Plunkett wobbled over to a cabinet against the back wall of the reading room and opened it to reveal a wall safe set into the dark wood. He spun the dial a few times and the safe opened with a pressured pop. He withdrew a black leather briefcase.

"Here," he said, placing the case in front of Daniel. "Take a look."

Daniel flipped the lid open and saw stacks and stacks of laminated newspaper clippings, Web articles, reports . . . They were all written within the last few years, and all dealt with the same thing—unexplained, miraculous occurrences within the sleepy little town of Noble's Green. There were also pictures of every one of the Supers. This was a file on Daniel's friends.

"It's all there if you have the eyes to see. Your friends act as if they can go about their business and no one will notice. But over the years, people *have* noticed, Daniel."

"You've . . . you've been spying on them!"

"I am a very wealthy man. I have the resources. Finding the right people to get me information was never a problem.

Oh, I rarely used the same person twice—a private detective here, a little bribe there. I didn't want anyone else to get the whole picture."

Daniel couldn't believe it. It was all here, pictures of the tree house, of Rohan and Eric, Louisa and Mollie. Of him, even.

"You had no right!" Daniel said.

Plunkett looked indignant and hurt.

"You know, if you would just listen, you might end up thanking me! All this time that I've been investigating your friends, I've also been protecting them. I've spent a lot of money bribing the right law-enforcement officials to close certain cases early, or to ignore certain reported sightings. I've got half the cops in this town convinced that the Air Force is using Mount Noble to test out secret aircraft, and I've got the rest thinking that your kids' supernormal activities are just the pranks of bored university students. But there is only so much that one man can do, and an old one at that. Believe me, it's been a full-time job keeping up with your friends!"

"What? So you expect me to believe that you are doing all of this out of the kindness of your heart?"

Plunkett hobbled back over to his chair. He scratched at his shriveled, bald head and sighed. "Funny you should mention it," he said. "Three years ago I was driving along a back road near the mountain when I suffered the first of what would turn out to be several heart attacks. I lost control of the car and wrapped it around an oak tree. When I awoke, the car was on fire. I couldn't move, I was so weak that I could barely speak and I was about to burn alive.

"Then someone tore the door off the car and lifted me to safety. He didn't open the door, *he tore the metal door off the car*! Despite the smoke and the flames, I saw the face of my savior that day. The face of a little boy."

"Eric," said Daniel.

Plunkett nodded. "Others might have dismissed what they saw as a hallucination, but I . . ." Plunkett gestured to the sketches on the floor. "Well, I've always believed in the impossible.

"It took me a long time to recover. While I was recuperating, I became obsessed with discovering the identity of my savior. I hired men and I began to follow the clues. I soon realized that there is something wondrous going on in Noble's Green, just like in my comic books! But there is also something terrible."

Plunkett reached into the briefcase and pulled a black envelope from the bottom of the pile.

"Go ahead," he said. "Open it. We both know what you'll find."

With trembling hands, Daniel peeled back the flap and pulled out the glossy photo within. It was a hazy picture, mostly shadow. But the shadow had a shape, and a name.

"The Shroud," whispered Daniel.

"So now I have a question for *you,* Daniel Corrigan," said

Plunkett, his eyes wide. "How is it that a creature from my imagination, a thing I drew to scare children over sixty years ago, is preying on the children of Noble's Green today?"

Daniel had no answer. He was speechless. He'd been so sure that Plunkett was the Shroud. He'd been sure that this was all just some game of cat and mouse. But now as he looked at the little old man in his chair, holding a cup of tea with palsied hands, he saw something he hadn't expected to see—Herman Plunkett was afraid.

"Why are you showing this to me?" asked Daniel, frustrated. "Why did you give me those sketches in the first place? If you're not the Shroud, then what do you want from me?"

"I gave you those sketches because . . . because I'm a coward. When you came to see me, I didn't know what to think; I panicked. So I played the fool for you. I hoped that you would see the sketches as a clue, and from your reaction I'd know whether I could trust you.

"I'm not the Shroud, Daniel. I'm just a sickly old man with too much money who is terrified of something he drew over half a century ago." Plunkett picked up the photo of the menacing shadow. "This photo, as well as another like it, was taken last winter at the Old Quarry, and the man who I hired to take it disappeared soon thereafter. I knew then that I had gotten close to solving the mystery—too close. I've since backed off, but I have learned enough. Enough that I can tell you now what is really going on in Noble's Green. If you think you are ready to learn."

"Go on," said Daniel. He had a sinking feeling in his stomach, but he had to know. "Start with the powers. Where do they come from?"

"I haven't the foggiest," said Plunkett. "Meteor activity? Aliens? Maybe it's genetic? Maybe your friends are the next step on the evolutionary ladder?" He chuckled to himself. "Maybe it's in the water, who knows?"

Daniel began to wonder if the old man wasn't just a little bit senile. "I thought you said you had answers?"

"To some questions, yes. But not the ones you want to hear. As best as I can figure it, this all started a few years ago. . . ."

"A few? But it's been going on for generations. What about the Rules?"

Plunkett shook his head. "I don't know anything about any Rules. But I can tell you that this is a relatively new phenomenon. Your friends are the first of their kind."

Daniel rubbed his eyes. It made no sense. Eric had told him that the Rules had been passed down for generations.

"The Shroud," said Plunkett, "is a more recent development."

Daniel stood up and began pacing back and forth. This was all just too much to take in. And why should he believe Plunkett anyway? He could be insane, or worse.

The old man went on. "Imagine the following scenario, Daniel: One day, for whatever reason, some of the children of this town start doing incredible things, magical things.

Some can fly, some are strong, some are fast. Now imagine that another child realizes that he has a power, too. Only this isn't a nice, shiny power like his friends'. He can't fly, he can't run super-fast; all he can do . . . *is steal other powers*. He's like a leech, this one. He can take the powers away from others, absorb them and make them his own. And what's more, when his friends lose their powers, they lose their memories of ever even having had them.

"Just imagine, watching your friends do all these wonderful things while you stood there, unable to join in. How long could you resist? How long before you took some of that power for yourself?"

Daniel stopped pacing. Plunkett's gaze was frightening, but Daniel couldn't look away. When next he spoke, his voice was sad, and the fear was gone, replaced by something like pity.

"It's not fair, really," said Plunkett. "A child shouldn't have to make that kind of choice, he shouldn't have to resist that kind of temptation. There are few adults strong enough, much less a little boy. Especially a boy whose head is already filled with dreams of superheroes. A boy whose dream world was formed by the four-color comic-book depictions of heroes and villains. The boy dreams his whole life of being Johnny Noble, only to wake up one day, alone in the knowledge that he is something else entirely. He's quite the opposite. He's the Shroud."

Daniel felt sick to his stomach. He looked down at the

stack of comics before him, the complete run of *Fantastic Futures, Starring Johnny Noble*. Complete except for two missing issues.

"Who?" asked Daniel, but the question had already left a bitter taste in his mouth.

Plunkett wiped his dusty glasses on his sweater sleeve, breathed on a lens and then wiped them some more. When he was finished, he answered with a question of his own. "Think back. What have you seen the Shroud do? What is it capable of, and who do you know that can do the same? You have faced the Shroud twice now, so who among you was missing each time?"

Daniel didn't answer, but Plunkett nodded anyway. The old man saw the understanding, the realization, in Daniel's eyes and that was enough. Daniel was thankful that Plunkett didn't make him say the name out loud, because to do so would have felt like a betrayal.

"There is one last picture in the envelope, Daniel."

Daniel reached in and pulled out the last photograph. In a kind of shock, he looked at it, took a deep breath and put it back. Then he sat down. He couldn't feel anything anymore. He was numb.

"If you value your friends, you have to find a way to stop him, Daniel. If you need proof to convince the others—more than the photograph, I mean—then find the missing comics. They were his inspiration—may God forgive me for ever drawing them. They gave him the idea for his disguise. He'll still have them. Find those comics and you've found the Shroud."

It was nearly dark by the time Daniel pedaled back home. The normally welcoming houses of Elm Lane tonight seemed menacing in the twilight shadows, and the brisk November breeze chilled him to the bone. He parked his bike beside Mollie's front yard and stared for a long time up at her window.

How can I do it? he asked himself, picturing the devastation, the heartbreak, in her eyes when he told her that they had to fight one of their own. He would know the look because he was wearing it right now. They had been betrayed, all of them. Betrayed from within.

He pulled the black envelope from his coat pocket and stared once more at the photo inside. It was grainy and showed a shadowy figure standing in a tangled thicket at night. Beneath the billowing blackness, beneath the dark disguise that was melting away, was a boy's familiar face.

How can we fight our friend? How can we fight Eric?

Chapter Seventeen
About Eric

Daniel decided to approach Rohan first. Although Rohan was close to Eric, as close as any of them, he was still consistently the most logical mind in their little group. It would be important to have him there when he told Mollie. Mollie was all action and reaction—strong, but also emotional.

Daniel still couldn't quite grasp the fact that he was planning a strategy to defeat one of his best friends. To beat Eric—their leader, and the strongest of them all. Daniel still hoped to reason with him, to somehow talk him out of all this madness, but he knew that they needed to be prepared if that failed.

The Shroud was one of their own.

As much as it sickened Daniel to admit it, Plunkett's version of events made sense. The Rules kept the younger Supers in line, kept them afraid. Eric could use the same lies on the kids near his age, like Michael, until he could get them out of the picture, until he could steal their powers, too. Now there were only a few left, and the only real threats to him, power-wise, were Mollie and Clay. Soon he wouldn't even have to hide. Soon there would be no one strong enough to stop him.

They needed to act fast. If Eric learned that he'd been discovered, he probably wouldn't have any problem attacking first. He could come for Mollie and Rohan anytime—even tonight! They needed to be ready.

When Daniel found Rohan, his friend was lying in the grass in his backyard with his ear pressed against the earth. His glasses were off and his face was pinched tight with concentration. He was so absorbed in whatever he was doing that he didn't notice, or didn't care, that his dog, Shaggy, was sitting next to him and contentedly chewing his way through Rohan's untied shoelaces.

And he's the "logical" one. . . .

Daniel approached Rohan and waited. Shaggy trotted up to Daniel and wagged his tail, a piece of Rohan's shoelace dangling from his mouth. Daniel scratched the mangy dog behind the ears and called, "Rohan. Hey, Rohan!"

Rohan did nothing.

Daniel sighed and lifted his foot. He brought it down on

the ground hard, and watched as Rohan jerked upright with a start.

"Ah! Earthquake!" he shouted. "Oh, it's you."

Rohan pulled his glasses out of his pocket and blinked up at Daniel. "I was listening to a new ant colony being built under Mom's rosebushes. You surprised me."

"Yeah, well. We need to talk. It's about Eric."

"Eric?" asked Rohan, standing. He absentmindedly dusted himself off. Rohan had a habit of dusting off all the wrong parts of his body. He usually patted down the clean patches and left the dirty ones the way they were.

"If you're worried about Eric," said Rohan, "don't be. It's all taken care of."

"What? What do you mean?"

"I mean that Mollie and I talked it over last night and we decided that you were right. You've been fighting too many of our battles for us, Daniel. It's not fair. So Mollie is taking care of Eric herself."

Taking care of Eric? Just how much did they already know?

"Wait a minute, Rohan. What are you talking about? What do you mean that Mollie's taking care of him? Have you been talking to Plunkett?"

"Plunkett? Of course not! I only meant that we decided to tell Eric about the Shroud and all that we've learned. He'll probably be mad at us for breaking the Rules, but his birthday is coming up and we felt like he should know the truth. We *owe* him the truth."

Daniel let go of his breath, which he hadn't even been aware he'd been holding, then sat down on Rohan's porch.

"Daniel, what's wrong? You don't look so good."

"It's Eric, Rohan. I think we've all made a terrible mistake. We need to go see Mollie before she talks to him. I have something to tell you both, and it will be easier if I only have to say it once."

"Before she talks to Eric? She's with him right now. She was going to see him this morning and tell him everything. I offered to come along, of course, but she wanted to do it alone."

Alone? Mollie was alone with Eric? Who knew what he might do once confronted with all she knew? Eric's birthday was only a few weeks away, and the way Daniel saw it, Eric would then have two choices—either he could pretend to lose his powers and his memory, thereby protecting his secret for a while longer, or he could decide that he was so powerful that he didn't need to hide anymore. If he chose the second option, he would want Mollie out of the way. All he would need was an opportunity to be alone with her. . . .

"Rohan! We need to get over to Eric's now! Mollie's in danger!"

"Danger? From what, the Shroud? She's with Eric, she couldn't be safer."

"No, she's in danger *from* Eric!"

"Who's in danger from me?" asked a voice from the sky above.

Daniel looked up to see Eric floating above them, Mollie by his side. Daniel had to shield his eyes as Eric drifted down, the sun shining like a halo behind him. It should have been one of those wondrous scenes, an image that Daniel would've remembered forever, but after what Daniel had learned it was horrible. His friend was something grotesque.

Rohan spoke up before Daniel could answer. "Eric, isn't it kind of risky to be flying around in broad daylight like that? And in my backyard, no less?"

"Aw, c'mon, Rohan. I flew so fast that no one would've seen me. I wouldn't have been more than a blur. I'm getting faster and faster every day!"

Yeah, thought Daniel sourly, *and I know why.*

"Sometimes," Eric said as he picked up Shaggy in a bear hug, "you just have to live your day like it's your last. Am I right, Daniel?"

Daniel looked at Eric, searching his face for some sign that he suspected something—a wink, or a sneer. But all he found was that smile, that contagious smile.

"Yeah, Eric. Absolutely."

"So, c'mon," he said. "Who is in danger from little old me?"

He met Daniel's look with an even stare.

"Mollie," Daniel answered. "She's in danger of losing her title of fastest flier. It's like you said, you're getting faster and faster every day."

Mollie snorted. "In your dreams, maybe."

"Well, thanks for the vote of confidence, Daniel, but I don't think I'll ever be that fast. The jealousy is just killing me."

"Well, that's what I meant, anyway," said Daniel.

Rohan gave Daniel a look. It was obvious that Rohan suspected that he was lying, but he didn't call Daniel on it. He seemed content, for now at least, to give his friend the benefit of the doubt.

Eric glanced around. "You guys want to go out to the fort today?"

Rohan looked anxiously to Daniel, who said, "Actually, I need to hang near the house. I promised my mom I'd help her sort through Gram's stuff."

"Oh," said Eric. "Sure, buddy. Of course. Rohan? Mollie?"

"I, uh . . . chores," said Rohan.

"Okay," said Eric. "How about you, Mollie? Care to do some flying?"

Mollie looked at Daniel, hard. Daniel returned her stare, and prayed that his eyes told her all she needed to know.

"Maybe later," she said at last. "I might meet you there."

Eric shook his head, visibly disappointed. "All right. You know where to find me if you change your mind. Bye, all."

And like that, he was gone. True to his word, he was so fast that they could barely see a flash as he sped off into the sky and into the shadow of Mount Noble.

As soon as he was gone, Mollie turned on Daniel, poking him in the chest. "Do you guys mind telling me what's going on? You look like you've just swallowed your tongue, Rohan."

"Daniel has something he needs to tell us, Mol. Something so important it's worth lying to Eric for. At least it better be."

Daniel sighed. He had a bad taste in his mouth already.

"Mollie, what did you tell Eric? Did you tell him about the Shroud?"

"Well, no. I was going to but . . . I chickened out, okay? I was hoping we could tell him together."

"That was my first plan, Mol," said Rohan. "But you said you should be the one. . . ."

"Well, I changed my mind, okay?"

"Knock it off, both of you," said Daniel. They didn't have time for this, and Daniel couldn't put the truth off any longer. "I have something that I have to show you. When you see it, you'll understand why I lied to Eric. It wasn't easy, but I had to do it."

Daniel showed them Plunkett's photograph of Eric as the Shroud.

As it turned out, lying *had* been the easy part. The truth was much, much harder.

Chapter Eighteen
Briarwood

They took the news that Eric might be the Shroud about as well as Daniel had expected. Rohan's first reaction was to get very quiet. Daniel knew that he was turning the evidence over in his head, testing for himself whether Daniel's conclusion fit the facts. Rohan was quick to point out that photos could be altered. Heck, with a little time at the computer, he could make any one of the kids into the Shroud. But Daniel thought Rohan would eventually agree that they should at least look for more evidence, even though he would urge caution along the way.

Mollie's reaction was just as predictable, if a tad more violent. First she called Daniel a bad name and then she took a halfhearted swing at him, which he managed to duck. Daniel knew it was halfhearted because if Mollie really wanted to hit him, he wouldn't even see it coming. As it was, he barely got out of the line of fire in time, despite the fact that he was waiting for it.

Then Mollie got quiet, which in many ways was worse. Daniel would take the hitting and cursing Mollie over the quiet Mollie any day.

"But you don't have any real proof," she said after a time. "You have all these theories and Plunkett's word, but no proof!"

"There's the photo," offered Daniel.

"Photos can be fakes!" said Mollie. "Rohan just said so!"

"Listen," said Daniel. "I hope I'm wrong. I *pray* that I'm wrong, but you have to admit that Plunkett's theory makes a lot more sense than everything else we've been told. All that stuff about the Rules and Johnny Noble—do I even have to *ask* who first told you all of that?"

Mollie was silent, but Rohan nodded. "It was Eric," he said.

"Eric is older than all of you," said Daniel, "and he's only a little younger than the other kids who've lost their powers. From a strategic standpoint it makes sense—you go after them when they turn thirteen, before they get too powerful to stop. And just look at all the things Eric can do! He's as strong as Clay, he can fly like Michael could and he's almost as fast as Mollie. Why does he have all those powers when you all have, at most, one or two?"

"Then why does he wait at all?" asked Mollie. "Why doesn't he come after us when we're little, like Rose?"

Daniel hadn't thought of that but, surprisingly, Rohan had the answer. "Well, if what Daniel says is true, then maybe he wants the powers he steals to be strong. He waits just long enough for the powers to ripen, so to speak, but still acts before they become a real threat."

Mollie shot Rohan a look that spoke daggers.

"*If,*" he said, throwing his hands up in the air. "I said *if*!"

"Mollie, I don't want to judge Eric guilty without more proof, but I also don't want to find ourselves unprepared if the worst happens," said Daniel. "If it is Eric behind all of this, then it's because he's sick and I want to try and help him if we can."

Mollie kicked at a pebble with her shoe and stared at the dirt. She looked, for a moment, like a very little girl. It reminded Daniel of how out of their depth they all were.

"Okay," she said quietly. "What do you want to do?"

"Well, first of all, you were right—we need more proof. If we're going to confront him, then we need more than just conspiracy theories and a blurry photo to back us up. We need to find those missing issues of *Fantastic Futures,* the ones featuring the Shroud. If Eric has those in his possession, that's pretty strong evidence that he's been less than honest."

"Anyone up for a little breaking and entering?" asked Rohan.

The three of them stood outside Eric's window, trying to summon up courage that no one wanted to find. They were preparing to break into the house of one of their best friends. While they hesitated, a feral cat and her kittens skittered off under the house while a neighboring guard dog strained against its leash and barked a warning. Rohan pointed to a single beaten-up car in the driveway.

"Looks like someone's home," he said.

"Eric's mom," said Mollie. "She works the night shift at Norma's Grill, so she'll probably still be asleep."

Rohan gave Mollie a worried look.

"It's all right," she said. "She sleeps with earplugs in."

They parked their bikes by the side of the house and went around the rear, careful to stay out of reach of the barking dog. The yard reminded Daniel of lots back in Philadelphia— mostly weeds and dirt.

"Wow," said Rohan. "I never knew that Eric lived . . . like this."

"They're not rich, but they're good people," Mollie said. Even as she said the words, she grimaced. Daniel understood the struggle going on inside her—if they found what they were looking for, that would mean that Eric wasn't such a good person after all. It would mean that he wasn't even the person they thought they knew. This morning Daniel had taken Mollie's entire world and turned it on its head.

"Here," she said. "That's his window." It was just a few inches above the grass itself.

"He lives in the basement?" Daniel asked.

"It's not as bad as it sounds. You'll see."

Mollie knelt down and pointed to a latch that dangled

loose at the edge of the pane. "The lock's busted, and Eric uses it to sneak out at night. . . ."

Mollie suddenly fell silent.

"I didn't mean it like that," she said quietly. "That sounded terrible."

"We know," said Rohan. "We all feel the same."

Nodding, she pushed on the window's base, opening it inward.

Mollie stood up and dusted off her knees. "After you, detective."

Daniel eyed the window suspiciously, wishing that he'd thought to bring a flashlight. The sunshine would give him enough light to see by, but it was still pretty dark down there.

"Rohan, why don't you come with me? And, Mollie, you keep an eye out. Eric said he was going to the fort, but just in case."

"Don't worry. Just hurry up."

Daniel scooted through the open window, followed by Rohan. Both kids fit with no problem. Daniel noticed that the earth around the window was worn smooth. Eric must have used this exit a lot.

It wasn't as dark inside as Daniel had feared, and he took a moment to study the room. It was typical Eric—posters of superheroes and long boxes filled with comics everywhere.

On the opposite wall there was a map of Noble's Green and the surrounding countryside—one of those satellite photos taken from space. Daniel had seen the exact same kind in the observatory gift shop on the day that Eric had saved his life.

The day that Eric had saved his life . . .

There was that sick feeling again, the guilt knotting up Daniel's stomach like rope. "Let's hurry," he said to Rohan. He didn't want to be here any longer than he had to.

Rohan began looking through the comics while Daniel studied the map. As he looked closer, he saw tiny pinholes dotting the entire area. There was one pin for the Tangle Creek Bridge and quite a few more for spots here in Briarwood. Daniel suspected that Eric was marking all the places where he had actually done some good, all the places where he'd been a hero.

"I don't think you should bother with the regular comic boxes, Rohan. At least not to start. He'd probably keep these comics hidden away, so we need to find a hiding place. Like a locked box, or a secret compartment or something."

"Sure, I'll just pull on the candelabra and reveal the hidden passage that leads to his lair. The Shroud-Cave."

Daniel looked at Rohan.

"Sorry," said Rohan. "I'm a little stressed out."

"It's okay. Let's just get this over with."

They continued to search Eric's room, looking under the bed and behind bookshelves, but found nothing. Despite the frustration, Daniel actually found his spirits starting to rise— maybe Eric was innocent, maybe this was all just the paranoia of a lonely old man who'd read too many pulp novels.

He was just about to call it quits when Rohan returned to the map on the wall.

"You looked at this?" Rohan asked.

"Yeah. Looks like he's using it to record his adventures."

"But why is it breathing?"

"What? What are you talking about?"

Daniel joined Rohan at the map and followed his friend's eyes. Sure enough, the map was moving, ever so slightly. The surface undulated in a slow rhythm, like a sail in a light breeze.

"Hold on," said Daniel. He grabbed the edge of the map where it was taped to the wall. Careful not to tear the paper, he peeled it back and exposed the air shaft behind the poster. A very slight draft issued forth, causing the edges of the map to ripple.

The grating was missing, and the open vent went back into the wall before disappearing into a larger central shaft. Resting in the cavity was a small stack of comics wrapped in plastic. Daniel gently removed them from their hiding place and showed them to Rohan, who nodded. Then Rohan pointed to the window as Mollie, silhouetted against the sunlight, peered through it. Daniel held the books up to the light and showed her the dusty covers. There was no mistaking the shadowy figure drawn on the front.

She said nothing, but the look on her face was unmistakable. Daniel couldn't have hurt her more if he'd physically struck her.

"Mollie!" Daniel shouted. "Wait!" But it was too late. Mollie stepped away from the window and was gone.

That was when he heard the footsteps upstairs. Daniel looked at Rohan, who was shaking his head.

"Oh man," he said. "We are so grounded."

At that moment the door burst open and two policemen with flashlights appeared, brandishing pistols.

"Freeze!" one of them yelled. "Hands in the air!"

As Daniel put his hands up, he saw a woman peeking over the shoulder of one of the officers. She was in her bathrobe and had a cell phone clutched to her chest.

"My goodness," she said. "They're just kids!"

Yes, Daniel thought. *I wonder if they have kid-sized hand-cuffs? Because it looks like we're going to jail.*

Chapter Nineteen
Grounded

*J*ail, thought Daniel. *Jail would've been easy.*

At least in jail they don't give lectures. At least in jail you don't have to see the disappointment on your parents' faces. Sure, you might stare at bars all day, and your cellmate might be named Mad Dog, but all of that seemed like a pleasant alternative to Daniel. At least in jail he could hide from all the trouble he'd caused.

As it had turned out, Eric's mother wasn't really a deep sleeper after all, and when a helpful neighbor called to tell her that some people were trying to break into her basement, she woke up in a hurry. The police were quick to arrive, and she even offered the handsome young deputies cookies before they hauled the two juvenile delinquents off in the squad car.

As for Mollie, she had disappeared, and Daniel had a sinking suspicion as to where.

Daniel's mother didn't say much to him when the officers brought him home, his little brush with the law being just one more thing to deal with. This made Daniel feel worse than any punishment would have; with all the grief she was feeling right now, she shouldn't have to worry about him as well. She sent him to his room and said that they would deal with all this when his father got home, which was typical of the justice system around the Corrigan household. "Wait till your father gets home" was an old, familiar refrain.

In his bedroom, Daniel found a box of Gram's belongings that his mother had left for him. The last thing Daniel wanted to do right now was to go through a box of painful memories. But his mother wanted him to choose a few keepsakes and, considering the amount of trouble he was already in, he thought it wise not to push his luck.

As the day gave way to night, Daniel opened one of Gram's old scrapbooks. While he idly flipped the pages, dark thoughts took over and he found himself wondering if Rohan or Mollie would be receiving a visit from the Shroud tonight. Or would it visit Daniel instead? What would Eric do to him, now that there was no more need for secrecy?

Daniel came across a page of old newspaper clippings, yellowed with age. The headline of one in particular caught his attention—"Meteor Shower Expected to Follow Recent

Comet Sighting. Families Plan Comet-Watching Parties!" Dated October 12, 1934, it was practically ancient.

Next to the article was a child's drawing. Its colors were faded and the paper was wrinkled and torn, but Daniel could still make out the picture clearly enough. A girl standing next to a building on fire, stars falling out of the sky around her.

It was not the drawing of a happy child.

There was a knock at his bedroom door. "Daniel," said his father, opening the door. He hadn't waited for an invitation.

His father wasn't alone. There was a thick-necked police officer with him. Neither of them looked at all pleased. "Daniel, this is Sheriff Simmons, and he'd like to talk with you, son."

The tone of his father's voice set Daniel immediately on edge. He had expected his father to be serious, but there was something more going on here. There was something new in his father's eyes. Was it fear?

"Hello, Daniel," said Sheriff Simmons. "You mind if I sit?"

Daniel gestured to the desk chair, and the officer lowered himself gingerly onto the seat. Sheriff Simmons was not a small man and the chair protested under his weight. Daniel's father remained standing in the doorway.

"So I hear you had a little run-in today with a couple of my deputies?"

Daniel nodded.

"I hope they didn't scare you too much, but you know you

can't be going into people's homes without their permission. Even the homes of friends. You understand that, right?"

Daniel nodded again.

"Answer the man, Daniel," said his father.

"Yeah. I mean, yes, sir."

"And you also understand that we'd be curious as to why you'd do a thing like that? Why you'd go into your friend's room when he wasn't there?"

"I told your deputies. We were going to surprise Eric when he got home. We were just fooling around is all."

Daniel saw the sheriff glance over to Daniel's father and noticed the deep lines of worry creasing his father's brow.

Daniel's mouth had gone dry. "What's going on?"

"Well, that's the thing, isn't it?" said Sheriff Simmons. "We were hoping that you might be able to answer that question for us. You see, your friend Eric didn't show up for dinner this evening and, well, after what went on this afternoon, his mother is understandably concerned."

"He's . . . he probably just lost track of the time. I haven't seen him, though."

"Uh-huh," said Sheriff Simmons. "And how about your friend . . . Mollie Lee? That was her bike that we found with you two, wasn't it?"

"Mollie?"

"She's gone missing, too. She missed her afternoon piano lesson, and her parents expected her home hours ago. Any idea where she might be?"

"No."

"Maybe she's with your friend Eric? That possible?"

"I guess it's possible."

"Enough, Daniel!" snapped his father. Daniel had rarely heard his father raise his voice, but now his face was red with anger. "This is not a game! Those parents are worried sick, and if you know anything about what's going on, you'd better tell us right now!"

"I don't know where they are," Daniel replied. "I don't."

Sheriff Simmons gave Daniel a hard, long look. "You know what, Daniel? I believe you. But I also believe that you're not saying everything there is to say.

"I'm on my way to Rohan Parmar's house next," said the sheriff, standing. "But don't be surprised if I stop back for another visit before the night is through."

His father looked meaningfully at Daniel as he shut the door and said, "We'll talk later. Until then, you are not to leave this room."

And just like that, he was alone again. Eric was missing. Mollie was missing. The police were searching for both of them, and apparently he and Rohan were the prime suspects. Well, he doubted they were actually *suspects,* but the cops could tell that they were hiding something.

Were they ever. *Well, Mr. Sheriff, actually Mollie could be anywhere since she can fly, and Eric doubles as a power-stealing super-villain, so the chances are that if you find her, he won't be far off. . . . Glad I could help!*

It was all just happening too fast. He wanted to be *doing* something, to be helping Mollie or trying to stop Eric, but the problem was he couldn't leave his room. Not only that, but he didn't really know where Mollie was, or if she was even in danger. For all he knew, she might just be flying above their heads, letting off steam.

Something else was bothering him, too. Something that he had been thinking about just before the interruption. He had been looking at Gram's old scrapbook when a photo in there caught his eye. . . .

Daniel picked up the hefty book again and hauled it over to his desk. Under the light of his desk lamp, he could just make out enough detail in the rest of the faded old clippings to make reading them worthwhile. The book was oversized and a little unwieldy, with a cracked binding and dusty cellophane sheets protecting every page. As he thumbed through, Daniel's attention was drawn first to a photo of what could only have been Gram as a little girl. She was wearing her Sunday best, standing between a kindly-looking couple. There was a certificate attached to it, brown and faded with age. It read, "The great state of Pennsylvania hereby acknowledges the adoption of Eileen Stewart, aged ten, by Mr. and Mrs. Herbert Lewis. . . ."

Gram was adopted? This was a startling fact, one that Daniel was shocked he hadn't known before. But even more shocking was the newspaper clipping next to it. The article was dated October 14, 1934, just a few days after the strange comet had been seen in the skies over Noble's Green. The headline read, "Local Trapper Leads Miraculous Survivors of St. Alban's Fire to Safety." There was a photograph accompanying the article, a photograph that Daniel had seen before, hanging on the wall of the Mount Noble Observatory. Though the photograph was hazy and the newsprint dim with age, Daniel could still pick out the haunted eyes of the orphans of St. Alban's, nine children with their faces covered in soot. Standing in the middle was the trapper, Jonathan Noble. Daniel tried to study Johnny's picture in detail, but the photo was too old to glean much. This Johnny was bearded and even dirtier than the children he'd rescued. Still, there was something familiar about his face, the tilt of his head. Below the picture was a caption, which Daniel read with interest. It was a listing of all the surviving orphans. Daniel used his finger to scan the names, squinting to read each faded letter. There she was, standing just to the right of Jonathan Noble—little Eileen Stewart. It was remarkable to think that Gram had been an orphan, but to know that she had survived the St. Alban's fire was almost too much to take in. Daniel supposed he could understand why she wouldn't talk about that period of her life, but he still felt a little hurt that he hadn't known until now.

Daniel was just about to turn the page when something in the face of one of the other children made him pause. It was a little boy, smaller and scrawnier than the rest, and his eyes stared at the camera with an intensity that Daniel found alarming. Whereas the other children looked mostly exhausted and frightened, this little boy wore a strange, angry scowl. Daniel went back to the list of names. "Will Naughton . . . Mai Lee . . . Herman—"

"No . . . ," whispered Daniel. "No . . ."

But it was. Daniel knew those eyes, he knew that look. *Herman Plunkett, aged nine,* was looking up from the page and scowling at him. He was reaching across time, to scowl at the foolish, gullible boy who fancied himself a detective.

Just then something moved outside his open window. The blinds stirred in the breeze, before exploding.

Daniel just managed to duck out of the way as a shape came hurtling through the window. Pieces of plastic flew everywhere as the blinds came tearing down on Daniel's head.

The Shroud!

But it wasn't the Shroud. It was a girl—a girl who'd landed in his bed, who was covered in scratches and cuts. Her normally dirty clothes were even more filthy and torn.

"Mollie!"

"Hey," she whispered weakly, "New Kid." She looked as if she'd just flown through a wall.

"You're hurt," he said. "I'll get my dad."

"No! I'm fine. I just . . . need to catch my breath."

Daniel started to go anyway, but she grabbed hold of his wrist and wouldn't let go. "You were wrong, Daniel," she said between breaths. "About Eric, you were wrong!"

"Mollie, what happened?" he asked, coming back to her side. Now that he got a good look at her, she didn't appear to be seriously hurt. She was, however, a mess.

Mollie was talking, but Daniel couldn't understand what she was saying. She was in hyper mode, and her mouth moved so fast that it was little more than a blur to Daniel's eyes.

"Mollie, slow down. I can't understand you. Here, drink this," he said, handing her a bottle from the bedside table. "It'll help." Mollie took it and sucked down its contents gratefully.

"Ugh," she sputtered, catching her breath. "I hate apple juice."

"Yeah, well, it's wet. Mollie, slowly now. What's going on?"

She sat upright and rubbed at the dirt and grit in her eyes. She already seemed more herself, but Daniel noticed that she was keeping a wary eye on the window.

"I was with Eric."

"I kind of figured."

"I know, Daniel, but I needed to see him, I needed to hear the truth from him."

Daniel started to scold her; he almost opened his mouth to tell her how incredibly stupid she was, how she'd put herself in danger and caused everyone a lot of worry. But then he saw the look in her eyes, and for the first time he wondered— were Mollie's feelings toward Eric more than friendly? He knew that Eric was important to her, but now he began to wonder just how important.

"Go on," Daniel said.

"Well, I found him there, at the fort. And I told him everything. I hadn't planned to. I'd planned on weaseling the truth out of him, like they do in the movies, but once I started talking, it all just kind of burst. I told him about Simon, about the quarry, about Plunkett and, of course, about the comics you found in his room."

"And what'd he say?"

"He denied everything! I honestly didn't know what to believe because, Daniel, you should've seen the look on his face—it was like I'd hurt him. Real, real bad."

Mollie sank back onto Daniel's bed now, and when she next spoke, her voice was softer. "Then he went kind of crazy, I think. He kept going on and on about the real Johnny Noble and how *he* would know what to do. Then he just left. He flew off without a word."

"And you followed him."

"Well, duh! I wanted to see where he was going, even though by that point I had a pretty good idea."

"The quarry?"

"Yeah. He got there just as the sun was going down. Just one of these days I'd like to see that place in broad daylight. I bet it's not half as scary then. I was behind him. I stayed far enough back that he wouldn't see, and I watched as he went into that tunnel and . . . and . . ."

"What?"

"The Shroud was waiting for us. I was hiding near the entrance when all of a sudden it was there, on top of me. I couldn't breathe."

"The Shroud? But you said Eric went into the tunnel."

"That's my point, Daniel! We were wrong about him! We were so wrong."

"Okay. Okay. But if the Shroud caught you, how did you get away?"

"Eric! It was Eric! He came out of the tunnel like a

thunderbolt and started fighting! Daniel, he was really fighting—I've never seen anything like it! They tore up the whole quarry—rocks and dirt were flying everywhere. I thought that Eric was going to win, I really did, but the Shroud was just too strong.

"Then the Shroud saw me and I . . . I flew away. I left Eric there and I escaped, like a coward. But Eric is still alive. He was unconscious when I left, but he was still alive. We have to go, we have to help him!"

Daniel took a deep breath. He stood up and went over to the desk, where Gram's scrapbook was lying open. The picture of little Herman Plunkett stared back at him from that faded photograph.

"You're not a coward, Mollie. You couldn't beat him alone. The Shroud wanted you to see that Eric was still alive. He wanted you to go get help; he's taunting us. Without Eric, we have no chance of beating him, but he knows that we'll try. He's using Eric as bait so that he can end it all tonight."

"Daniel," said Mollie. "If Eric's not the Shroud, then the photo Plunkett gave you . . ."

"Was a fake. It was a lie, just like everything else he's been telling me. And I fell for it all. It's Plunkett. He's the Shroud and he has been all along."

Daniel looked out the window at the stars emerging in the early-night sky. His parents would be coming up here to check on him any minute now. The entire Noble's Green Sheriff's Department was out searching for Eric while he was caught in a life-and-death struggle with the true villain—a twisted old man who'd manipulated Daniel and preyed upon the children of Noble's Green for who knew how many years.

"C'mon," Daniel said, stepping to the window. "Are you strong enough to walk?"

Mollie nodded, but her eyes were worried. "Are we going to the quarry?"

"Yes. We'll pick up Rohan and the others along the way. Plunkett wants a fight, then he'll get one."

"But what do we do when we get there? You said yourself that we're not strong enough to beat the Shroud."

"No, but I know someone who is," Daniel said, his jaw tight with determination. A plan was forming in his head, an outrageous plan that only a fool would try. . . .

"So," he said, a smile forming on his lips. "Feel like taking a trip to the junkyard?"

Chapter Twenty
Strange Alliances

The most unnerving thing for Daniel's gang so far had been all the patrol cars. It was strange to see the police driving along slowly, searching the shadows with their high-powered floodlights. Worse still was the knowledge that the police were searching those shadows for *them*.

They spotted the first car as they were leaving Rohan's house. As Rohan scurried down the tree that served as his bedroom escape ladder, they watched the car disappear slowly in the distance. By the time they saw the next one, Daniel's parents would have noticed that he was missing, and Rohan's disappearance might have been noticed as well. When they saw the third car, there was probably an all-points bulletin warning that half the children of Noble's Green were gone. With Louisa and Rose now in tow, Daniel couldn't help but feel like the Pied Piper in the fairy tale, leading the village children off into the hills, never to be seen again.

As it was, they certainly didn't look like a fairy tale—five children on bikes, skulking along the edge of the woods. Rose wanted to stop and pee every ten minutes, and of course she was scared of the dark. Daniel would have liked to leave her out of this, but she shared a bedroom with Louisa and had threatened to tell their parents if she wasn't allowed to go along. So Louisa rode with Rose on her bike and encouraged her to hold her bladder. Along the way they explained everything to Louisa, who listened attentively but said little. Daniel knew that she had probably figured out much of it on her own anyway, but he didn't miss her shocked look when they got to the part about Eric's capture. Again he felt his face burn with shame. But in the end she made no judgments, she offered no reprimands. She was as good as her word— they were her friends and she was going to stick with them.

It was left to Daniel to lead the way, which was ironic, as they were headed to the last place he'd thought he'd ever be trying to find.

It didn't take long for Daniel to locate the torn hole in the chain-link fence. He lifted the loose flap of fence so the others could squeeze through.

"Shouldn't we be worried about night watchmen? Or guard dogs?" asked Louisa, looking over her shoulder.

"Guard dogs?" repeated Rose worriedly.

"I don't think anyone cares enough about this old junk-yard to use guard-anythings. All we've got to worry about is Clay and Bud."

"They're enough," said Mollie.

Once they were safely inside the fence, Daniel again took the lead. "Okay, Louisa, you hang back a little with Rose. You know how unpredictable Clay and Bud can be."

"Bud stinks," offered Rose.

"Yeah, so you should have no problem staying back with your sister. And no disappearing unless Louisa tells you to, okay? We don't want to lose track of you in this junkyard. It wouldn't be good for the mission."

Rose saluted. In an effort to stop her constant whining, they had told the five-year-old that they were all on a top-secret mission, which delighted Rose to no end. Now every little request was met by a salute.

"You be careful, Daniel," said Louisa. "Clay is dangerous."

"Trust me, I'll be fine." Daniel remembered the pounding that Eric had received from Clay in their fight. He swallowed hard.

"Rohan, can you tell if they're here?"

"Well, if Bud's here, there's one easy way to tell." Rohan closed his eyes and sniffed the air. He immediately made a sour face.

"Oh yeah. They're here," he said. "Ugh, and one of them is smoking a cigar!"

When they found Bud and Clay, they were sitting in a

stripped-out old van that was covered in graffiti. In several places the phrase "Bud Rules" shared space with "Clay's Hideout—KEEP OUT!" The doors were missing and the windows were all broken out. A small camping lantern hung from the ceiling, and the two boys were sitting on either side of a makeshift poker table. Clay was chomping and coughing on a noxious cigar.

"Your bet," he spat as foul brown saliva trickled down his chin. "See me or fold."

"Um, I'll . . . see your bet and raise you."

"You can't raise me."

"Why not?"

"Because that's the rules! How many times do I have to explain everything to you?"

"Well, I might listen better if I didn't have you blowing that smelly thing in my face all night long!" said Bud, waving away the oily smoke.

"Smelly? Look who's talking, stink-butt. This stogie is the only thing that's keeping me from puking all over the place!" Clay coughed. He took a long drag on the cigar, but his face was turning green with the effort.

"Yeah, well, those things'll kill you."

"I'll still live longer than you unless you shut up and bet!"

Watching the two of them bicker, Daniel wondered if he and his friends could stand there all night and never be noticed. Those two might have been mean, they might have been tough, but they were about as observant as a couple of bricks. Unfortunately, time was wasting.

"Hey, Clay. Hey, Bud," Daniel said. It sounded weird, even to his own ears, saying hi to those two. But he had to start somewhere.

The two bullies looked at Daniel, their mouths dropping open. Daniel saw Clay quickly scanning the faces of the gang behind him. Daniel knew who he was on the lookout for.

"What the heck are you all doing here?" asked Bud. "Clay, what the heck are they doing here?"

"Shut up, Bud," Clay answered. He laid down his playing cards and stepped out from the van, his eyes warily searching the yard around them. "You're not welcome here, New Kid. None of you are."

"It's no great thrill to be here," said Mollie, holding her nose. The smell of Clay's cigar was quickly being overpowered by the acrid stench of Bud-stink.

Daniel shot Mollie a look before going on. "We're not here for trouble, Clay. We're here to ask for your help."

"My help?" Clay looked around suspiciously. "Why?"

"I don't have a lot of time to explain, but—"

"Hey, wait a minute. Where's your little leader? Your little bodyguard, Eric?"

Daniel took a breath. This was it, this was the tricky part.

"He's . . . he's in trouble. That's why I came to you, because Eric's in trouble and we need your help to save him."

Clay studied Daniel for a long moment. He was searching Daniel's face, looking for a hint that this was all some kind of joke, some kind of trap. When he spoke next, it was with a mean smile. "You know what? I believe you."

He stepped forward and planted himself directly in front of Daniel, breathing cigar smoke into his face. Daniel's eyes watered and he choked back a cough, but he held his ground.

Clay leaned close. "I also believe that you just made the biggest mistake of your life coming here."

Daniel could hear Bud laughing a few feet away, and he could see Mollie, in his periphery, taking a step forward. Daniel waved her away without taking his eyes off Clay.

"You might be right, Clay. But let me ask you one question before you beat the stuff out of me—when do you turn thirteen?"

Clay's smile disappeared immediately. "That's none of your business, New Kid."

"I bet it's not too far off. You're big for your age, but you've gotta be at least twelve, right? What are you going to do when you turn thirteen? Who will you push around then? Why, I bet even Bud'll be able to take you. Then it'll be *Bud's* Hideout. You'll just be his toady."

Clay gave a snarl and shoved Daniel. It was more of a nudge, really, but nevertheless it sent Daniel skidding onto his back.

He heard the commotion as his friends began to move between him and Clay.

"No!" he shouted. "Everyone stay back! Clay's not going to hurt me!"

"Oh yeah?" spat Clay, but he did stop. "Why shouldn't I pulp you all right here and now?"

Daniel sat up and rubbed at his chest. He imagined the

hand-shaped bruise that would be there tomorrow. That is, if he survived tonight. "Because, Clay Cudgens," said Daniel, "if you help us rescue Eric, you'll be able to stay strong for the rest of your life. It doesn't have to end."

Clay squinted at him while chewing on his soggy cigar. Daniel slowly pulled himself to his feet and brushed himself off, trying not to wince when he touched his chest. Clay took a look around at the others—at Louisa's and Rose's fearful expressions, Rohan's unreadable stare and Mollie's angry glare—then looked back at Daniel.

"Talk," said Clay. "You've got five minutes."

"It's all I'll need," Daniel said. "But first, do me a favor and put out that stupid cigar."

Chapter Twenty-one
Back to the Mountain

They were about three-quarters of the way to the Old Quarry when Daniel began to wonder which would turn out to be more dangerous—facing the Shroud in its lair or simply getting there. None of them really knew what to expect when they finally faced the Shroud as a group. Despite Clay's cocky bravado (he'd been loudly listing the many forms of violence he planned on using against the villain), Daniel knew that it promised to be a terrible fight. But as it turned out, biking along the side of the road in the middle of the night had its dangers, too. Though traffic was scarce along the old Route 20, there was still the occasional logging truck or pickup. With each approaching car, the glow of distant headlights would send the kids scrambling for the trees, ditching their bikes and jumping for cover in the thick brush or (as often as not) thorny brambles. Daniel feared that they'd landed in a patch of poison ivy at least once.

Still, despite the occasional panicked retreat, they were making good time. They had a few flashlights between them, which they used to light their way, and though Clay's bragging was an annoyance, it did keep them from dwelling on their fears. For that reason alone, Clay was proving to be a valuable ally—he was so irritating that everyone forgot to be afraid.

Mostly forgot, anyway. Daniel knew that in the back of each kid's mind, there was a voice whispering that some of them might not make it back home tonight. Daniel knew this because the voice was practically screaming in his own head. Plunkett's plans for the children were still a mystery, but it was clear that for some reason he hungered for their powers. His motives concerning Daniel were less clear. And now that Daniel knew the truth, he was a threat to the old man. Just how far was Plunkett willing to go to eliminate threats?

"Then I'll grab a tire iron and wrap it around his scrawny little neck," Clay was saying when Daniel started listening again.

"Really?" asked Rohan. "And I suppose you thought to bring along a tire iron for this very purpose?"

"You know, I could always use a little Buddha kid instead," said Clay.

"Hindu, Clay. If you're going to use my religion as a derogative, at least get it right."

"A deroga-what?" puffed Bud from several feet away. The plump Bud had trouble keeping up with the other kids, for which they were very grateful.

Daniel listened to the banter between Rohan and Clay for a while longer, then stepped up his pedaling and pulled ahead. Mollie was leading the pack. Her bike was apparently in police custody, so she'd had to borrow one from Louisa. It was bright pink with white pom-poms that dangled from the handlebars. Very un-Mollie.

"Hey," he said, catching up to her.

"Hey," she replied. One look at her face and Daniel could see that she was barely paying attention to the road—Mollie's attention was focused on the stars.

"You know," she said, "I could be there right now. I could be there in the time it takes for Clay to mispronounce another of his stupid insults."

"Of course you could, but then we'd just have to rescue two kids instead of one. We've been over this. If we even have a shot of beating the Shroud, we have to work as a team."

Mollie gritted her teeth, but she didn't object. Daniel knew that she was fully aware of the Shroud's power, and of her own limitations.

"He'll be okay," Daniel offered. "Eric will be okay." But even as he said it, he heard the doubt in his own voice.

Mollie nodded, but Daniel could see the tension in her face, in the set of her jaw. By this point they were well ahead of the other kids, but no matter how fast they pedaled, it wouldn't be fast enough. After a moment she said, "Daniel, we still don't know . . . I mean, what *is* Plunkett? Is he a man? A monster?"

"I think he's a little of both. I don't know how he got the way he is, but I'm willing to bet that it had something to do with the St. Alban's fire."

"You're talking about that old newspaper clipping you found."

"Yeah. Plunkett was one of the orphans that Noble saved that night, and the orphanage burned down the same night some kind of comet appeared in the sky."

"A comet? Do you think that has something to do with all this?"

"Yeah, well, I just have this feeling. I have this *sense* that the two things are wound up with Plunkett in all of this. And I intend to find out."

Mollie was quiet for a moment. Then, "Daniel? You said this was in your gram's scrapbook?"

"Yeah?"

"So she was a survivor of this fire? Along with Jonathan Noble and Herman Plunkett?"

Daniel gave Mollie a hard stare. He knew what she was about to suggest, but he didn't want to think about it. Not now. It was just too terrible.

"Daniel," Mollie pressed on. "We can assume now that Plunkett was lying and that there have been Supers for years. For generations. What if it all goes back to the fire like you think? What if those kids, along with Johnny, were the first—the first generation of Supers? What if your gram . . . was a Super?"

If Mollie was right, then Plunkett had stolen his gram's powers the same way he'd stolen Simon's, Michael's. . . . He'd stolen a lifetime of miracles.

"She never really talked about her life as a kid," he answered. "If you're right, then Plunkett didn't just steal her powers, he stole her childhood. He deserves to die." Daniel was silent for a moment. "This is all my fault."

Mollie gave him a sideways look. "How so?"

"Plunkett was afraid of Eric. Plunkett couldn't be sure of beating him in a fair fight, so he used me to get to him. And I bought every lie. Believed every story. It's because of me that Eric walked right into that trap, far away from home, from help.

"And you know what the worst part is? I think a part of me was anxious to believe Plunkett's lies. Looking back at everything Plunkett told me, there were all kinds of holes in his story, but I didn't even question them. I think I was . . . I *am* jealous of Eric and of all the things he can do. Jealous of the way that you, that all of you, feel about him. It felt good to be the center of attention for once, to . . . to lead. So I cut my friend off from his team, turned you all against him, and then sent him out there to face the Shroud alone. It's all my fault, Mollie."

Mollie said nothing. For what seemed like an eternity, she just pedaled along, lost in her thoughts. She wouldn't even

227

look at Daniel. He knew that she must be even more disgusted with him than he was.

"You know," she said, braking her bike to a complete stop, "you make me want to scream."

"Um, huh?"

"Look at me, Daniel Corrigan, because I am only going to say this once—this is not your fault. This, all of this, is the fault of Herman Plunkett, or the Shroud, or whatever he wants to be called. He fooled you. He fooled all of us. For years he's been fooling us.

"You say that you're jealous of Eric—well, join the club. You don't think Rohan wouldn't rather pick up a car, or fly, instead of listening to bugs digging all day? You think I wouldn't give anything to be strong enough to punch stupid Clay Cudgens in the face the next time he mouths off to me? We are all jealous of Eric. But we all love him, too, and I know the same goes for you. Tell me that your heart didn't break when you thought he was the Shroud, and tell me that finding out that you were wrong doesn't feel just a little good?"

Mollie put her hand on Daniel's arm and looked him in the eyes.

"You've just been through a terrible experience, Daniel. Losing your grandmother . . . it's something that I can't imagine going through. It's gotta be so bad to feel so . . . so . . ."

"Powerless?"

Mollie smiled. "Yeah. But you're not. You're smart and you're brave. You didn't give up on Simon, and I know you won't give up on Eric. He's your friend and he needs you. We all need you."

Mollie leaned in close to Daniel, so close that he could feel her breath on his cheek. Her face was only inches away from his.

"But if you don't stop feeling sorry for yourself, I am going to punch *you* in the nose," she said, and Daniel could see that she meant it.

"Hey, Daniel," interrupted a voice behind them. "Did you see that shooting star?"

"Huh?" Daniel turned to see Louisa pedaling hard to catch up. Rose clung tightly behind her, and the rest of the gang followed them.

"Oh. Hi, Louisa. No, I didn't see anything."

"Why are we stopped?" asked Rohan. "Something wrong?"

"No," answered Daniel, red-faced. "Just waiting for you to catch up."

"Daniel," continued Louisa, "you should have seen it! It was directly in front of us, a flash in the sky . . . there it is again!"

Daniel looked up to where Louisa pointed, and this time he did see something. It was like a streak of fire, but it was traveling low, far lower than a comet or shooting star should be. And it was coming toward them.

"Wow," cooed Rose. "Pretty."

"Everyone off the road!" shouted Daniel. "Find cover!"

But it was too late. No sooner had the words left his

mouth than Daniel found himself flying off his bike, blinded by a thick cloud of dirt and debris. Something had struck the ground very near them, and that something was laughing.

Daniel recognized the voice—a deep, hoarse whisper. He tried to call out to his friends, to warn them or to make sure that they were okay, but his mouth was full of sand and his ears were ringing from the impact. Tiny flashes of light dotted his vision and a sharp, biting pain was rising in his bad arm, which was twisted awkwardly underneath him.

Wiping the dust from his eyes, he looked up just in time to see a shadowy figure pounce on top of him. Strong fingers, like the grip of an iron vise, dug into his shoulders, and his head began to spin as he was lifted into the air. Daniel screamed, but his voice was drowned out by the sound of coarse laughter. The last thing he saw before losing consciousness was the ground disappearing beneath him, littered with the bodies of his friends.

Chapter Twenty-two
The Cave

When he came to, the first thing Daniel was aware of was the pain. It was a familiar throbbing agony that originated in his left arm and washed over him in waves. The second thing was the cold. This being November, there was a chill to the evening air, but this cold bit like a deep winter freeze. Rough stone scraped against his face. The air smelled wet, like earth.

Daniel stretched his fingers out into the darkness. There were none of the faint shadows or telltale shapes that you might find in a dark room. This was a darkness that was total, absolute. Daniel brought his good arm up to his face and waved his fingers in front of his eyes to confirm his worst fear—he was blind.

"Do you know where you are?" asked the darkness.

Daniel froze and listened to the voice—raspy like crinkling sheaves of old paper—a voice he knew and feared.

"Plunkett?" Daniel asked.

"Yes, Mr. Corrigan?" The voice was close. He could be standing right over Daniel and Daniel wouldn't even know.

"I can't see."

"I know. But you haven't answered my question—do you know where you are?"

"How can I know where I am if I can't see?"

Daniel heard Plunkett—the real Plunkett this time, not the muffled whisper of the Shroud—give an exasperated sigh, but Daniel didn't care. He was focusing all his might on keeping the panic out of his voice, even as the encompassing darkness threatened to swallow him whole. He was fighting the claustrophobia brought on by the blindness, and concentrated on keeping his breath even, steady.

"You have other senses," said Plunkett. "And you have deduction, reasoning, as well. Now I repeat—do you know where you are?"

Daniel forced himself to relax, and he stretched out both arms into the dark. Instantly, he regretted it as a burning pain raced up his bad arm. Plunkett's attack had undone weeks of delicate healing that had gone on beneath the cast—the bone had snapped a second time. He winced, but he managed not to cry out.

"Ignore the pain. Fight through it," said Plunkett.

He reached out again, this time with only his good arm,

and felt the ground he was lying on. It was definitely stone—cold and rough. He could hear the slight echo of dripping water nearby.

"We're in the quarry. Behind your secret stone door."

"Very good. And do you have any thoughts as to what else might be behind my secret door?"

Daniel gritted his teeth and forced himself to breathe. What was Plunkett up to with all these questions? Was he just playing more games—toying with his prey? At least this game was buying Daniel time. Every minute that he kept Plunkett talking was a minute Daniel stayed alive, and increased his chances of finding and freeing Eric. So he buried his anger and fear, and let his deductive mind get to work.

"I suppose that it's something you want to keep hidden, something important to you. . . ."

"Yes?"

"And before this was a quarry, it was the site of the St. Alban's orphanage, wasn't it? Before it burned to the ground. Before the night the comet appeared over Mount Noble. . . ."

"Call it by its real name, boy. *Mount Noble* is a meaningless honorific. The ancient tribes who first settled in its shadow called it by a different name—Witch Fire Mountain! Noble had nothing to do with the secrets of this ancient place." There was a sudden change in Plunkett's tone, a defensiveness that hadn't been there before. So Jonathan Noble was a sore spot for the old man.

"But otherwise, your deductions were splendid," continued the darkness. "A top-notch bit of reasoning."

Daniel's vision exploded in a field of white, of shooting stars. It was more than a blindfold being ripped off his eyes—it was darkness itself peeling away from his eyelids. The pain was excruciating.

When his vision cleared, his now-tender eyes focused immediately on his adversary—Herman Plunkett, the Shroud. He was sitting across from Daniel in a very different chair from the overstuffed recliner in his library. This one was made of stone and earth, and it appeared to be dug out of the very cave wall. Plunkett was playing with a strand of darkness, the same cold darkness that had just been peeled from around Daniel's eyes. It was thin, like a fine filament string, yet fluid—ebbing and flowing between Plunkett's fingers. There were other strands of the stuff here and there about Plunkett's body as well—the remains of Plunkett's villainous Shroud disguise.

Plunkett merely watched as Daniel examined the rest of his surroundings. As he'd suspected, he was in a limestone cave. Daniel could feel the cool wind of a draft upon his face. A kerosene lantern provided feeble light, enough to see by at least. But the shadows swallowed up everything beyond this small patch of light, so there was no telling how deep the cave went or how tall its ceiling was. Daniel could see well enough, however, to make out Eric's body lying a few feet away. His friend was breathing softly, easily, but was unconscious.

Behind Eric was a small alcove, into which was set the massive rolling door that Daniel had seen from outside. It was, of course, sealed tight.

And the walls were covered in pictures. They were etched and stained into the very stone—scenes of battle, of hunting and of worship. The artwork was primitive and reminded Daniel of the cave paintings in Europe he'd seen pictures of at school. These paintings were better preserved, though, and in most places the color was still vibrant, the detail remarkable. These paintings had been hidden from the elements, and from prying humanity, for many years. Behind Plunkett's chair was another kind of mural, a collage of photographs—framed and hung with care from the rocky wall like family pictures in a hallway. Such a modern affectation looked out of place in this ancient cave.

"They tell the story of this mountain," said Plunkett, gesturing to the painted walls. "This place had stories many thousands of years before our ancestors walked its forests. We are such a funny race, humans. Compelled to scratch our lives out in ink, on paper or rock. Whether it's a limestone wall or the pulp pages of a comic book, I suspect it's hardwired in our DNA—the urge to record our lives."

Daniel said nothing, but he thought of the drawings that lined the walls back in the tree fort. Generations of extraordinary children who'd scribbled down a record of their lives in pencil and crayon.

As if reading Daniel's mind, Plunkett pointed to the

framed photographs behind him. "These are my humble contributions to history. A wall of remembrance for those who came before. My Hall of Would-be Heroes."

Daniel squinted at the photos, and though it was too dark to see any details from where he was lying, one thing was certain: they were all pictures of children. Generations of children.

"So you collect . . . what? Pictures of your victims from over the years?"

"Victims? Hardly. I saved each and every one of these children. I saved them from themselves."

"So, we *are* in Mount Noble . . . I mean, Witch Fire Mountain?"

"Yes." Plunkett smiled. "Resting comfortably in the belly of the beast." That turn of phrase sent a chill through Daniel. He didn't like to think about resting in the belly of anything.

"And what about my friends?" Daniel asked, remembering the sight of their bodies strewn about the ground. "Are they all right?"

"They are fine. They were a bit stunned by my grand entrance, but no permanent damage was done. In fact, I believe they are on their way to rescue you even now."

Daniel let go a sigh of relief and with it his greatest fear—that his friends had been hurt, or worse, in the confrontation with the Shroud.

"Interesting move, recruiting the Cudgens boy to use against me. Here I have taken away your king," said Plunkett, gesturing to Eric's still form, "and you go and move one of your pawns to replace him. That took first-class strategic thinking."

Plunkett leaned in close, his creepy smile wide. "Do you play chess, Daniel?"

"Yes."

"Good. I'm glad my metaphors, at least, aren't wasted on you."

"*Wasted* on me? What are you talking about? You kidnapped me, attacked my friends. . . ." Daniel knew that he might be pushing it too far—he feared the anger lurking inside the old villain—but he couldn't stop. These games had gone far enough. "Why don't you end all of this?"

To his surprise, Plunkett just smiled. "You are burning with questions, aren't you? Always the detective, even to the bitter end. I like that about you. Very well, ask away. I will indulge you with an answer or two. You will find that I can be generous when it suits me. Ask."

"Okay, then—who are you? I mean, really? Are you Herman Plunkett . . . or the Shroud?"

"Where does Herman end and the Shroud begin?" Plunkett said. "Is the Shroud Herman's secret identity or is Herman the Shroud's?"

Plunkett chuckled, and Daniel squirmed at the sound of that laughter. There was a frayed edge to the old man's voice that had been well hidden until now. "So everything you told me was a lie. You lied to me and framed Eric for it all."

"Not everything was a lie. I told you what you needed to

know, and fed you the information that suited me and my purposes. It's true that I used you to turn your friends against each other, but it was necessary, I assure you. The special children of Noble's Green were no match for my power—until you showed up and began uniting them against me! I couldn't have you all standing together. So I manipulated you to get you and your friends away from Eric, and without his strength the rest of your friends will be little bother. Even with the help of the Cudgens boy.

"I brought you here, in part, to say thank you."

Daniel bit back the urge to tell him where to put his "thanks." Instead he decided to press him for more information. "What is this place?"

"A hidden network of caves that runs throughout the mountain. They were used as homes by the primitive peoples many thousands of years ago. Most collapsed long ago. This one was uncovered only by chance by the quarry company, which I own, of course."

Plunkett sat back in his chair, his face practically breaking with that smug grin of his. That smile made Daniel sick to his stomach. Still, there had to be some value in keeping him talking. Plunkett had at least revealed that Mollie and the others were on their way to rescue him, though they did not seem to worry the villain in the slightest. It was up to Daniel, then, to discover something that they could turn to their advantage. Daniel's fascination with Sherlock Holmes came from Holmes's mastery of the details. Holmes viewed every situation as a giant puzzle, and the details that ordinary people missed were often the pieces that put it all together. If he kept Plunkett talking, perhaps the old man would reveal something that Daniel might use against him, something in the details. . . .

"So, you own the quarry. Which, basically, means that you own most of Mount Noble. . . ."

Plunkett made a sour face at the mention of Noble's name, but he nodded.

"But why?" Daniel asked. "What use are a bunch of cave paintings if you are just going to hide them from the rest of the world?"

"Think it through, Daniel. You've seen the paintings — these caves are a history, they are proof."

"Proof of what?"

"Proof that this has all happened before, and it will all happen again. The storm is coming, Daniel, and we must be prepared to meet it." Plunkett chuckled. He was making less and less sense, and Daniel began to wonder if the old man was finally slipping into total madness.

"You said that some of what you told me at your house was true," said Daniel. "I saw your photograph. You were at St. Alban's, but you were just a boy."

"Correct. The brothers of St. Alban's took in unwanted children from all over the world. Those street urchins and cast-offs who were lucky enough to be rescued by the brothers were given a new life at the orphanage.

"I was the unluckiest of those lucky few."

Daniel decided to try out a few guesses to keep the old

man talking. "And when St. Alban's burned, Johnny Noble rescued you from the fire?"

"Also true. Johnny saved the children of St. Alban's. I watched it all happen; I witnessed how all the great gifts were bestowed that night. When the meteor struck the orphanage, the whole place was consumed in green flame—the color of a distant star. It moved like a thing alive! And it killed without mercy, a witch fire.

"It would have taken the children, too, if not for Johnny. Stupid, lucky Johnny—a dumb backwoods trapper who saw the fire fall from the sky and ran in to help. Without a second thought, he charged into that inferno and emerged . . . different.

"It was something in the smoke, I think. Something that got in their lungs. It could not kill them, so it changed them. It transformed them all."

The old man's face contorted with rage. "All but one! All but Herman Plunkett! Poor, picked-on Herman, who was hiding in the outhouse when the meteor hit. Poor Herman, who escaped the flames and missed his chance to become a god."

Daniel was afraid of the white-hot anger in Plunkett's eyes, but he had to go on. There was a question that he had to have the answer to.

"And my gram?"

Plunkett's rage instantly dimmed, and his shrunken little body sank in his seat. For the first time, he seemed unwilling to meet Daniel's gaze. "Yes. Her power was the strongest of them all, next to Johnny's, of course. When she flew, Daniel, you should have seen her. She shone so bright—like the sun. . . ."

Daniel pictured Gram lying in her bed—so sick, so frail. "And you took it from her!" he said through gritted teeth. "You stole it all away!"

"NO!" shouted Plunkett, on his feet. "Not her! I mean . . . I didn't mean to. It wasn't my fault!"

Plunkett began pacing back and forth now, wringing his hands as he went. The little trails of darkness followed his every move.

"You have to understand, at first I didn't know how to control it. And I would never have done that to Eileen if I'd known then . . .

"I was never a popular boy, and of all the orphans at St. Alban's, she was the only one who showed me a bit of kindness. I was . . . fond of her."

Plunkett's eyes grew distant again as he remembered. "I saw what they could do. They emerged from the fire changed, all of them. I watched as they used their powers, hesitantly at first, then bolder and bolder each day. It was only a matter of time before they were discovered. Noble disappeared soon after the fire, the coward, and he left behind a dangerous legacy. Unchecked. All that power in the hands of children. He abandoned them. He abandoned *us*!

"And it was only my bad luck that I wasn't one of them. I became obsessed, I admit it. I stalked the old burned-out ruins of the orphanage for some answer, some clue as to how or why this had happened. Eventually my obsession paid off. In the rubble I found a black stone, a piece of the actual meteorite that had ignited the fire! I was ecstatic at the time; I suppose I hoped that the stone might give me powers like the others'. I nearly broke my neck jumping from trees with that stone clutched in my hands. I nearly burned myself alive trying to re-create that magic fire, but nothing worked. All I got for my troubles were bruises and singed eyebrows.

"The disappointment was just too much. I went to Eileen and broke down in her arms. She had continued to be kind to me, even though I was more an outcast than ever. She even took me flying, Daniel. . . ."

Plunkett stopped now and wiped at one of his eyes. He had a faraway look on his face, and his mouth was twisted horribly. Whatever he was remembering, it was tugging at the old man's soul.

"I didn't mean to do it. One minute Eileen was holding me and the next . . . she was lying on the floor. She was breathing, but her skin was so cold. But *I* was . . . I was . . . filled with flame!

"It was the meteorite, you see? In my desperation I showed her the stone, and when she touched it . . .

"The meteor gave her those powers, and the meteor took them away—and gave them to me! The stone acted like a kind of siphon. Eileen's power came to me through the stone, only it changed. Rather than being filled with a bright light, I was consumed by darkness, my darkness. And it did whatever I wanted it to.

"When Eileen awoke, she had no memory of what had happened to her, or of her powers. The powers protect their secrets well, and when they left her, they took her memories with them. But I now had a secret of my own.

"Over the next few years I discovered that I needed to replenish the powers of the stone every so often. It needed to feed so that I might stay strong. The other children of St. Alban's would have grown up to become menaces to society. Bullies with the power of gods. I took it upon myself to prevent such a tragedy. One by one, I took their power for my own.

"But in time he returned. After years away, Johnny Noble returned to Noble's Green. Somehow he knew what I'd been doing, and like a delinquent father he dared to come here and tell me to stop! He didn't understand what I was trying to do, how I was saving the world. He dared to oppose me, to lecture me like I was still a grubby little orphan child! But with the stone, I now had powers of my own.

"We fought here on the slopes of the mountain. Johnny was so much more powerful than I'd expected. That first generation of Supers, as you call them, was much stronger than those milksops you call friends. The powers have scattered and spread over the generations. Eric here is remarkable because he can fly and possesses strength, the Lee girl has speed to accentuate her flight, but back then there was no limit to the powers a single child might have.

"You cannot imagine how strong Johnny was. He was a grown man, and since I'd only ever fought children, I underestimated him. In the end, I lost. I barely escaped.

"After that defeat I resolved to hide and plan. I would face Johnny Noble again and this time I'd be ready for him. Unfortunately, I didn't get the chance. The Second World War began and Johnny left for Europe. He never returned. I don't know if he survived the war or not, but I never saw him again, regardless.

"I started the comic books as my personal revenge fantasy, but in time I found that it gave me great satisfaction to dream up Johnny's exploits and to profit off them. When you came to see me bearing those old books, well, the irony was just too delicious to ignore."

Daniel made a face at the memory of that encounter. "So all because of a meteor? A meteor hits and Noble's Green instantly becomes a town full of super-children?"

Plunkett glowered at him. "No, I did not say that. The meteor that struck St. Alban's was certainly part of the Witch Fire Comet. The alien energy from that comet changes humans, somehow. The phenomenon is rare, and though certain children continued to display abilities similar to the orphans', none of the succeeding generations were nearly as powerful as the first. I don't know exactly how these powers are passed on. A recessive gene, perhaps. It's a mystery I've yet to solve."

Plunkett rubbed his chin and frowned. The fact that some things about this place still baffled the old villain gave Daniel a small bit of satisfaction.

"So the Rules and all of that," Daniel said, pressing him further. "That was all you?"

"Of course," answered Plunkett. "Without Johnny to

stop me, my path to power was assured, but I still needed order, a way to control the children while protecting my secret. And how else do you control a group of rowdy children? You give them rules to follow."

"But in the end you became a villain, not a hero."

"I am the earth's greatest *hero*!" shouted Plunkett, startling Daniel. "For seventy years I've kept this world from being overrun by these menaces. Imagine a world where the children were allowed to reach adulthood with all that power. Even this pathetic, weak batch. Imagine what kind of damage Clay Cudgens could do as a grown man."

Daniel pointed to Eric's still form lying on the floor. "Eric isn't Clay. He's a good kid, and all he wants to do is help people."

"That's true today. But what about tomorrow? Or next year? Or the year after that? Eric has yet to suffer jealousy. What will he do the first time he has his heart broken? What kind of man will he be then? We both know something of poor Eric's family. All his life, men have bullied him, pushed him around. What happens the day he decides to push back?

"Real life is not a comic book, Daniel. And we are all better off with Johnny Noble dead. This world doesn't need superheroes."

"No, just you," Daniel muttered, and immediately regretted it. He wondered if the old man might strike him. But the moment passed, and Plunkett soon let out one of his cackling chuckles.

"You try and test me, but I know that I'm right," he said.

"We are like Holmes and Moriarty battling wits! But will our struggle be our doom, I wonder? Will tonight be our Reichenbach Falls?"

Plunkett removed an oil lamp from its sconce. Shining its light on the far wall, he pointed to the paintings there. "You see, Daniel—this has all happened before! Look! Look close, boy, and tell me what you see."

Daniel squinted in the gloom, and looked at what appeared to be the scene of a battle. Armies with spears and knives, fighting an enemy from above.

An enemy from above . . .

"They're . . . they're flying," said Daniel.

"Yes. The tribes here fought a war that could not be won, against the very gods themselves." Plunkett walked along the wall, illuminating the illustrated scenes as he went. "The Witch Fire they called it, a fire from the sky that burned the mountain. It came only once in many generations, and only the very eldest of them would live to see it twice. They thought it was an evil spirit that lit the sky and burned the forests, scaring away the game that the tribes depended on for survival. Finally, one year a generation of young warriors set out to meet the spirits of the Witch Fire in battle. The meteor fell from the sky and twenty young men marched out to meet it. Seven returned. And they came back changed. They left as boys and they came back something . . . more. The seven young warriors started out as protectors, but as they grew older, they became enemies of the tribe. Of all tribes.

"In time, they destroyed an entire people because no one was strong enough to challenge their power. In time, they destroyed themselves. That is the secret of the mountain, Daniel. But it's more than the past—it's the future that I am trying to prevent.

"By studying the cave paintings, and by studying the geology of this place, I've calculated that the Witch Fire Comet, or Spirit, or whatever it is, returns to this place every seventy or so years."

Daniel did the math quickly in his head. "That means that it is . . ."

"It's coming back. And when it does, we must be ready."

"We?"

Plunkett nodded, his voice softening. "It is presumptuous of me to think that I can defend this world alone. I am an old man, and though the power of the stone has granted me the strength to live a long life, no one is immortal. Every man must leave behind a legacy. When the sky lights up with fire again, there will be born an entirely new generation of superbeings, but they will be more powerful than the weak, diluted children of today. They will be like the gods of old—pure, strong and dangerous."

Plunkett reached into his sweater pocket and withdrew a small ring. It looked as if it were carved from coal, but there was a slight emerald sheen to it in the lantern's light. "With my powers, it was an easy thing to make myself a rich man. The company that dug this quarry was just one of many that I owned. A limestone quarry was simply a convenient cover for the real work going on here, the real quest. We dug this quarry not to search for limestone but to find this!"

"What is that?" Daniel asked, though he already knew the answer.

Plunkett fingered the ring. "It took years of digging, and many millions of dollars, to scrape together enough fragments of meteorite from the layers of rock and earth just to fashion this ring. A second weapon to defend against the future." Plunkett held out his hand, the ring glittering in his palm. "But it was worth it, so that I might have an ally, a successor."

"That's what this is all about?" asked Daniel, incredulous.

"You're the perfect choice. You're smart, brave. And, most importantly, *you are not one of them*! You're an outsider, just like I was. I never had a family and there is no one to carry on when I am gone. Fate brought us together, and you can't fight fate, Daniel. Fate has delivered to me Eileen's grandson, and together we will keep this world safe. You will come to understand the wisdom of what I do and why I do it.

"I'm offering you a greater gift than has ever been offered. You can finally fly, Daniel. With time, you will be able to do anything."

Daniel stared at the ring in Plunkett's hand. It was as if someone had taken the ground out from underneath his feet, and he was dizzy, poised to fall, with only Plunkett's words holding him up.

"What will it do?" Daniel asked, his voice barely a whisper. "Will it make me be like you?"

"No, Daniel. It will make you like *him*," Plunkett said, pointing to Eric's still form. "All of his power will be yours, if you are brave enough to take it."

Daniel hardly heard the stone door moving behind him; he was only dimly aware of the sound of Mollie's voice calling his name from somewhere far away. For the last three months Daniel had watched his friends do the impossible. He'd flown with them, played with them and even occasionally fought against them—all the while weighed down by the knowledge that he'd never be like them. Daniel knew what envy was—it was the ugliest of emotions, Plunkett was proof of that—but until now he'd been able to keep his hidden deep down. It was easy when you had no other choice. But now here was Daniel's chance to be special, to be more than the new kid, to be powerful. . . .

Daniel reached out, and Plunkett dropped the ring into his palm. It felt cold and heavy in his hand. But he didn't put it on. He just stared at it, and beyond he was aware of Eric's helpless form stirring in the dark.

"Good, Daniel," Plunkett said as tendrils of darkness slithered around the old man's body. The blackness flowed out from a burning ball of green flame beneath his sweater, and its tentacles snaked through the folds of his clothing and wrapped around him until he was, once again, a living shadow.

"Now," he said in the Shroud's throaty whisper, *"it's time to show your friends what real power is!"*

Chapter Twenty-three
Reichenbach Falls

Mollie was the first to act, of course. It was a predictable move, not just because of her speed but because of her anger. Daniel knew that she would be itching for a rematch and that first blood would belong to her.

The Supers had insisted that the Shroud fight them in the open—that much at least was good planning. They had no desire to face Plunkett in the shadows and confined quarters of the cave, and Plunkett seemed willing to oblige. He flew out of the tunnel like a shot, his eerie laughter echoing off the quarry walls, but thanks to Rohan, the Supers were ready. No sooner had Rohan shouted his warning than Mollie pressed her attack. She aimed for his legs, and at the speed she was moving, it must have felt as if he'd been hit by a car.

Knocked off balance, the Shroud tumbled down the hill to the bottom of the ravine, where Clay was waiting for him. Clay's first punch sent the Shroud soaring through the air, slamming him against the quarry's stone face. As the shadowy villain slumped to the ground, Bud started laughing, polluting the air with his sour stench.

"Look at that, Clay," giggled Bud. "You clocked him with one punch!"

Clay spat into his hand and wiped it on his dirty jeans. There was a dark sheen of something stuck to his knuckles. "Yeah, but it was like hitting an oil slick. Thought you guys said this guy was going to be tough." Clay turned his back on Plunkett and glared up at the rest of the group. "You losers were scared of *that*?"

"Don't turn your back on him! Stick to the plan!" shouted Rohan, but it was too late. There was a hissing noise, a rustle of movement, and from the Shroud's crumpled body, a long tendril of darkness spun toward Clay, lassoing his neck like a noose.

"*Strong child*," whispered Plunkett. "*Now it's my turn.*" The tendril twisted as the Shroud floated up into the air, and Clay's face turned blue with the effort to breathe. Bud was no longer laughing.

"Time for Plan B," shouted Mollie.

"What's Plan B?" asked Rohan.

"Hit him! Hard!"

She flew at Plunkett again, but this time he was ready. She struck a wall of blackness that tangled around her arms and legs. She might just as well have flown into a tar pit.

Bud was next, his cloud of noxious gas engulfing the Shroud, but to no effect. Whatever the Shroud stuff was made of, it protected him from Bud's attack.

From the entrance of the cave, Daniel watched as the Shroud took down the Supers' two offensive fighters. Without Clay or Mollie the battle was over; the rest of the group just didn't know it yet. As Daniel watched, Louisa appeared next to Mollie, phasing right through a boulder to reach her. She was trying to free Mollie from the tarlike blackness, but she seemed to be making matters worse as the clinging stuff spread over Mollie's body, almost as if it had a mind of its own. Bud and Rohan were desperately tugging at the noose around Clay's neck, but to no avail—Clay was strong and nearly indestructible, but he was gasping for breath that wasn't there. Even he couldn't last much longer.

And through it all, Daniel did nothing. He turned his back on the battle and walked back into the cave, to sit by Eric's side. Already the color was returning to his friend's face, and his breathing was getting stronger. He'd live, but by the time he woke up, it would be too late. The Shroud would have already won.

"All of this," Daniel said softly. "He's doing all of this because of me. Because he thinks I'm like him. I'm so sorry, Eric. They're going to lose and there's nothing I can do to help. I'm not like you—I'm no leader. All my plans led us here, right into his hands. Now he's going to win and I'm powerless to stop it." Daniel opened his fist, exposing the coal-black ring cupped in his palm. "Unless . . . unless . . ."

"Unless what?" asked a small voice behind him.

Daniel turned and looked for the speaker, but no one was there.

"Rose?" he asked. "Is that you?"

"I'm not supposed to say," answered a voice from nowhere. "Louisa told me to stay disappeared and to be quiet until it was all over."

"Run home, Rose. You should run home as fast as you can."

"But Louisa said—"

"It's too late, Rose. We lost."

"Aren't you going to help them? What's in your hand? Is it something to help them?" asked Rose, suddenly visible by Daniel's side. She was reaching for the ring in Daniel's palm.

"No!" he said, pulling his hand away from her. "You can't touch it! It'll hurt you if you do. I'm sorry, I just . . . I just don't know what to do!" But even as Daniel said it, he knew that it wasn't exactly true. He had the ring.

"Please!" shouted Rose, tears filling her eyes. "You're the smart one! Louisa always says! So help them!"

Daniel gripped the ring so tightly in his fist that he could feel it cutting into his flesh. The ring was an incredible source of power, but power at what cost? He might be able to use it against Plunkett, but first he'd have to use it against his friends.

Incredible source of power . . .

Then the answer hit him like a bolt from the sky. He felt that familiar rush, the excitement that he got when the final piece of a puzzle came together.

"Stay here, Rose, and look after Eric. You're right, I am the smart one, and I just figured out how to beat him!"

Shoving the ring into his jeans pocket, he ran along the tunnel, out into the open and toward the battle. He felt smart, he felt brave and he felt ready for a fight. Plunkett had made a mistake—one so obvious that Daniel had almost missed it. The old man had lived in a world of comic-book villains for too long.

"I know how to beat you!" he cheered as he bounded down the steep incline, careless of how much he stumbled or fell.

The Shroud looked up, and Daniel could feel the old man's angry glare from within that cowl of shadow. *"Don't be foolish, Daniel. This is your moment as much as it is mine."*

The ooze stopped its spread over Mollie. Rohan and Bud seemed to be making headway in freeing Clay. Apparently Plunkett's traps needed his full concentration to work, and if nothing else, Daniel had just bought his friends a little more time.

"You're going too far. You're out of control!" said Daniel.

"Sometimes sacrifices have to be made," said Plunkett. *"But you can save their lives, Daniel, by taking their power for your own and ridding them of their memories of all of this. Leave them powerless, or watch as they suffer the ultimate fate!"*

Plunkett wasn't bluffing, Daniel could tell. The years of secrecy and loneliness had finally driven the old man insane. For all these years Plunkett had deluded himself into believing that he was acting for the good of the world, while somewhere in the twisted recesses of his mind was the knowledge that he was really just a villain. The truth was there in his art, in those comics he had drawn so many years ago, in which he reduced himself to a lurking shadow, preying upon the sleeping, the defenseless. He wanted Daniel to help him continue the lie. He needed an ally to keep him from facing the truth, and he was willing to kill to get one.

"You said it yourself, Plunkett," said Daniel, taking another step toward him. He needed to keep Plunkett talking—to keep him distracted until he could get close enough for what he had planned. "You told me that Gram was full of light. She might've changed the world, but you stole that from her. I won't steal that same gift from my friends. I'm not like you and I never will be."

Though Daniel couldn't see the expression on Plunkett's face, he still felt the old man's fury. His rage was like a living thing, palpable in the very air around him. *"If you want to honor your grandmother's memory so,"* he hissed, *"then you can join her!"*

Daniel ran headlong at the Shroud, but only made it a few feet. From within the darkness of the Shroud's being came another tendril of blackness, whipping around Daniel's neck with an iron grip. But unlike Clay, Daniel wasn't invulnerable. He had no super-strength to protect him. With just a flick, Plunkett would snap Daniel's neck.

"Goodbye, Daniel. Such a waste. The world's greatest detective has just met his end."

Just then, the earth seemed to crack open. With a thunderous crash, the quarry erupted in a shower of wind and dust, blinding Daniel and driving him to his knees. When his vision cleared, he saw that he was free of the Shroud's tentacle and that Plunkett had engaged a new enemy. It looked like a scene drawn by the old man himself, an epic battle between the Shroud and his archenemy, Johnny Noble. Only it wasn't Johnny Noble—it was Eric.

Daniel had never seen anything like it. Though Eric was obviously still somewhat dazed, seeing his friends in danger had unleashed a new rage in him. Black tendrils lashed at his face and hands, but he shrugged them off, oblivious to the bloody red welts they left on his body. Through an act of sheer will, he fought his way past Plunkett's defenses, and when the two superpowered beings collided, the entire quarry shook with violence.

Daniel heard someone call his name, and he turned to see Mollie and the rest of the group scrambling over the rocks to reach him. They were all there; even Rose had appeared in their midst. Clay was conscious, and Daniel found some amusement in the fact that it was Rohan who was helping him limp along.

"Daniel, are you all right?" asked Mollie, her voice barely audible over the sounds of Eric's furious fighting. Daniel nodded, his eyes locking on the struggle raging nearby. "We have to help Eric!" she shouted. "He won't be able to keep this up for long."

Rohan was saying something, but his words were lost in the cacophony around them.

"What?" Daniel yelled.

"I said," shouted Rohan, moving closer, "that we need to get out of here. This quarry isn't as stable as it looks, and the fighting is going to bring the walls down on top of our heads. I can hear the rumbling already!"

"We can't leave Eric!" said Mollie.

"We won't," said Daniel. "I promise."

The tide was turning. Strong as Eric was, he was clearly no match for the Shroud's powers, and he was weakening fast. "Clay!" said Daniel. "Can you still fight?"

Clay shrugged and spat, "Yeah, I heal pretty fast. I was just a little light-headed is all. That creep jumped me while my back was turned." But for all Clay's bluster, he still seemed wobbly on his feet. Daniel hoped that the bully-turned-ally would be strong enough to last at least a few rounds against the Shroud.

"What's the plan?" asked Rohan.

"The plan is that you and Bud take Louisa and Rose to safety. Your powers aren't going to help against the Shroud."

"And what about you?" asked Rohan. "You don't have any powers at all."

"No, but I figured out Plunkett's weakness. Besides, I owe it to Eric. Now get out of here! We'll join you when we can."

Rohan looked as if he were ready to argue, but in the end he just nodded. When he turned to gather up the troops, he noticed that Bud was already halfway up the trail. "Didn't have to ask *him* twice," Rohan muttered.

Louisa surprised Daniel with a quick kiss on the cheek. "Be careful." Daniel hoped that the grime on his face sufficiently covered his blushing. One look at Mollie told him that it didn't.

Rohan led the others after Bud, and Daniel wasted no time watching them go. "Here's what we do. Clay, you need to get in there and help Eric. Then, while Plunkett's distracted, Mollie—I need you to get me as close to him as you can."

"Why?" Clay asked. "What can you do?"

Daniel allowed himself a small grin. "It's always in the details. Plunkett slipped up and told me the source of his power; now I just have to take it from him."

"Tell me," said Mollie. "I'm faster."

"No," said Daniel. "You can't touch it, either of you. If you do, you'll end up like Simon. It's gotta be me."

"Well, New Kid, you're no coward, I'll give you that!" Clay said, cracking his knuckles as he talked. "As for me, time for round two!"

Then Clay Cudgens ran down the side of the ravine to join the fight. No longer on the defensive, the Shroud had Eric cornered against the rock wall of the quarry. Large chunks of limestone fell around them as they traded blows. Daniel worried that soon Eric would be unable to defend himself; then nothing would prevent Plunkett from stealing Eric's powers and adding them to his own.

Mollie let out a low whistle as Clay blindsided the Shroud and brought him tumbling to the ground. "I never thought I'd say it, but I'm glad Clay Cudgens has our backs."

It was an all-out scrape now as the three of them tumbled and rolled across the quarry floor. In the kicked-up dust and gravel, it was hard to tell the combatants apart. Meanwhile, an ominous rumbling had become audible to even Daniel's ears. Pretty soon the whole quarry was going to come crashing down around them.

"Okay, Mollie," said Daniel, putting his arms around her neck. "The next opening you see, go for it! Fly me straight into him."

"Are you sure about this?"

"Not at all, but it's the best chance we've got."

Mollie wrapped her arms around his waist and smiled, but her eyes were glued to the scene below.

Daniel didn't have time to respond, because at that moment the Shroud let out a fierce shout of victory as he threw his enemies to the ground. He brought himself to his full height, the black tentacles of shadow forming into long, jagged spikes above the heads of Eric and Clay.

Mollie reacted quicker than lightning. She flew so fast that Daniel hardly had time to register any movement at all. One moment he was standing on the hill holding on to her, and the next he was hitting what felt like a wall of bricks. Layer upon layer of the thick shadow stuff flooded his vision as he struggled to keep from suffocating in the dark.

But Daniel knew that there was a solid body underneath that darkness—Plunkett's body. As the Shroud, Plunkett had the strength to snap Daniel in two, but it took concentration for those powers to work, and Plunkett was currently busy with Mollie, who was delivering a flurry of punches at lightning speed. Though Mollie's blows did little real harm, Plunkett was momentarily knocked off balance from the sheer ferocity of her attack. Hopefully, a moment would be all that Daniel needed, because a moment was all that he would get.

Daniel groped in the dark, searching for the Shroud's burning heart. His hands found the fabric of Plunkett's sweater. The answer was in the details, and the most important detail about Plunkett's powers was that they came from an outside source—the meteorite stone. Plunkett had fashioned one stone into a ring, but Daniel hadn't noticed any rings on Plunkett's fingers. That meant that he wore his stone in some other way, around his neck perhaps, near his chest. . . .

There was a sudden hiss as Plunkett realized what Daniel was searching for. They were soon locked in a fierce wrestling match—Daniel's hand closing in on Plunkett's throat as Plunkett tried to get a grip on the boy to throw him off. Pain shot up Daniel's bad arm but he ignored it; he willed himself to keep moving, his fingers to keep searching, clawing at the collar of Plunkett's shirt. . . .

And there he found it, strung on a chain around the old man's neck. Daniel's fist closed around the smooth stone pendant in the center of that ball of fire. It burned his hand but he refused to let go. He tugged hard, but the chain held. Daniel's breath was being forced out of him as the viscous blackness pressed into his mouth and down his nose.

He's drowning me, Daniel realized. *He's drowning me in shadow!*

Daniel's lungs burned and his stomach retched as the oily stuff seeped down his throat. His head started swimming and his eyes began to glaze over with a different kind of darkness. He was losing consciousness, and soon he would lose his life. Just as he was gathering his remaining energy for one last pull, he felt arms around his waist tugging at him, lending him their weight, their own strength. There was a deafening rumble, but he couldn't tell if it was the sound of the walls falling in or the blood pounding in his own ears. Like a human chain, the fighting children of Noble's Green pulled together, and Daniel felt a snap as the stone yanked loose in his hand, as the world collapsed around him with a roar. The ground seemed to open up beneath him and, together with his enemy, he tumbled into blackness.

Chapter Twenty-four
The Way Home

Daniel remembered a feeling of weightlessness and the sound of distant voices calling his name. He wanted to tell the voices to go away, that he was too tired to get up, but the voices were insistent as the weightlessness gave way to the return of gravity and the feeling of soft earth under his back.

When he opened his eyes, it was still dark, but now it looked as if someone had poked tiny pinpricks into the blackness. He was looking up at a field of stars, at a clear night sky. It was a welcome sight.

"He's coming to," said a girl's voice to his left. "Daniel?"

"Give him a moment," whispered another.

"Man, he fainted just like a girl."

"Shut up, Clay."

A girl leaned over him and stroked his hair. He was surprised to see that it was Louisa. "Daniel, how are you feeling?"

"Um, okay, I guess. Did we win?"

"Look around you," she said, smiling. Rose, Rohan, Eric, Clay, Bud and Mollie were all there. Most of them were grinning, too.

Daniel sat up too fast and his vision threatened to go blurry again.

"Careful," warned Rohan. "You were out for a few minutes. You're bound to be a little woozy."

Daniel propped himself up on his good elbow and rubbed his eyes. "Where's Plunkett?"

Rohan gestured over his shoulder. "He's down there. Somewhere."

With Rohan and Louisa's help, Daniel managed to stand and look around. He was on the grassy hilltop overlooking what was once the old quarry. Now it looked more like a giant sinkhole, filled with dirt and slabs of solid limestone. A dust cloud had risen from the destruction and was being carried away on the north wind.

"The whole thing pretty much collapsed," said Rohan. "You all were lucky you escaped in time."

"The stone? Plunkett's pendant!" Daniel said, remembering.

"It's down there, too," Mollie answered. "After you tore it off Plunkett's neck, his powers disappeared. His shroud—all that shadowy stuff—just faded and all that was left was this little old man. When the place started to fall apart, Plunkett ran for his cave. I don't think he made it. The last I saw, the ground was opening up underneath him, and he fell."

"That crazy monster was just an old geezer, can you believe it?" chortled Clay. Daniel knew he should feel grateful to Clay for his help, but the kid's careless reaction to all of this irked him too much. Daniel's plan had been to leave the old man powerless, not dead, and death was never a cause for laughter. Not in Daniel's book.

"I told everyone not to touch the stone, so we left it down there," said Mollie. "It's buried under a ton of rocks now."

"That's a fine place for it," said Daniel.

Daniel looked for the first time at Eric, who was bruised and beaten up. One eye was swollen shut and he was covered in wounds. "I owe you an apology, Eric. This is all my fault because Plunkett convinced me that you were the Shroud. I should've trusted you."

"Yeah, you should have . . . ," said Eric. "But Plunkett fooled everybody. Heck, he had *us* believing in those stupid Rules. For all these years I was convinced there actually was a Johnny Noble!"

"But there is!" whined Rose.

"Rose, quiet now," said Louisa. "I'll explain all this later."

"No! Johnny Noble is real! I met him when he helped Eric."

A sudden hush came over the group. It was Louisa who

broke the silence. "Now, Rose, what did Mom tell you about making up stories?"

"It's not a story!" Rose said. "Eric was sleeping, and during the fight Johnny Noble appeared in the cave and woke him up! He fixed him and then he flew away—faster than even Mollie. But first he told me to tell Daniel something. Something real important."

No one said anything—everyone was looking at Daniel.

"Johnny said to tell you that Plunkett didn't know as much as he thought he knew. He said that there are more answers out there, for a good detective to find."

"Eric," said Rohan. "How *did* you wake up? Just in the nick of time, too."

"I . . . I don't know. I just woke up. I heard the fight outside and, well, you all saw the rest. I don't remember anyone else around, though."

"It's true! I'm not fibbing!" shouted Rose, stamping her feet.

"It's okay, Rose. We believe you," said Louisa, giving the rest of them a look.

"No, you don't. But you'll see. Johnny Noble is real. For really real."

Daniel looked at Rohan, who just shrugged, and then at Mollie, who rolled her eyes. He remembered all that Plunkett had told him in the cave, about the real Johnny and the children of the fire, but he didn't say anything. After all the lies Plunkett had woven, Daniel wasn't sure what to believe, and it didn't feel right to be filling his friends' heads with more false dreams.

"Clay," said Eric, changing the topic. "I want to thank you for what you did. You really surprised us all."

"Yeah? Well, you can take your thanks and shove it! I wasn't here for you bunch of losers, I was here for me!" He leaned in close and practically growled, "Clay Cudgens is going to be the top dog in this town for a long, long time!"

He turned and started the long trek back home, with Bud nipping at his heels. He hadn't gotten far when he stopped and turned back. "You know what? I really should be thanking *you,* because I think I got something really great out of this whole mess. I got over my fear of heights.

"Things are gonna change around this place," he said with an ugly grin. "I promise." Then he turned and disappeared into the trees.

"Boy, does that kid know how to spoil a happy ending or what?" asked Rohan.

Eric looped his arm around Rohan's neck. "We'll handle Clay Cudgens. Just like we always have."

"I guess we'd better think about getting back, too," said Mollie. "I'd offer to fly someone, but I'm a little pooped."

"Yeah, me too," agreed Eric.

"So we bike home the old-fashioned way. Anyone want to place a few bets on who'll be grounded the longest?" asked Rohan.

"My mom's gonna kill me," said Mollie.

"Are you kidding?" said Daniel. "The sheriff was over at my house! I'm an outlaw!"

"Yeah, but I've been missing the longest," bragged Eric.

The Supers of Noble's Green went on teasing each other for the next mile, until they encountered another patrol car with its flashing red lights. Only this time they didn't bother to hide.

Chapter Twenty-five
The Legacy of Johnny Noble

"There goes one."

"Where?" asked Eric, squinting to see.

"There, just above the tree line." Daniel pointed. "See where the handle of the Little Dipper dips down? It was right there."

"That was a plane," said Rohan.

"Are you sure?" Daniel asked Rohan, who just blinked in response. "Okay, okay. But I'm making a wish on it anyway, just to be safe."

"Can you wish for it to be a little warmer?" asked Mollie. "I'm freezing my butt off!" To illustrate her point she let out a long breath and watched as it turned to mist in the chilled night air.

"Here," said Eric, offering her his mug. "Have some more hot chocolate. It'll warm you up."

"Thanks," said Mollie. "Want some, Rohan?"

"Sure," said Rohan. "But watch the backwash."

The four of them sat on Eric's front porch under a clear December sky. The temperatures had dropped steadily in the last few weeks, but they were still anxiously awaiting the first real snowfall of the year. With no snow on the ground, they had to satisfy themselves with other occupations like normal meteor showers and the pleasure of each other's company.

Other than at school, the Supers of Noble's Green had seen very little of each other over the last month, due to the mass groundings that came out of the night at the quarry. When the group of friends turned up at the police station, all dirty and bruised and bloody, their parents had been nearly hysterical. Once they realized that all of the children were safe and accounted for, their hysteria turned to relief, then to anger. The kids told their parents the truth, as far as they were able. They said that they had been afraid when Eric went missing and had decided to search for him themselves. They found him trapped in the old quarry (that alone was an offense punishable by a monthlong grounding), and the children went to rescue him. It was close to the truth, but blurry enough to still be a lie. Not one of them felt good about it, but they all agreed that there were just some secrets that grown-ups were not ready to hear.

And so there was no mention of Herman Plunkett or dark caves or any of that. In the end, Daniel suspected that the adults were actually a little impressed with the friends' loyalty, even if they were absolutely furious with their bad judgment. The punishments were severe, but each child sat through the lectures and the groundings with the secret knowledge that they had accomplished an unspoken good—friends had been saved and their futures were brighter than ever before.

It was now early December and their groundings would go on awhile longer, but four of the kids had been given a special one-day reprieve. After all, a boy turned thirteen only once in a lifetime.

"So," said Daniel. "What was your favorite gift?"

"Daniel! You can't ask Eric that!" chided Mollie.

"I thought the remote-control plane was pretty cool," said Rohan.

"That one was mine," said Daniel with a smile.

"The gifts were great, guys, but I'm not really thinking about presents tonight."

Eric put his arm around Daniel's shoulders and smiled. "I'm thinking about how lucky we all are that this new kid moved to Noble's Green when he did."

"Yeah," said Rohan. "Some things are just meant to be."

It was surprising how good it felt, to be one of them—to belong. At that moment, sitting with those three remarkable friends under a beautiful night sky, he knew that Eric was wrong—Daniel was the lucky one.

"You guys are going to make me throw up birthday cake all over this porch," said Mollie.

"All right!" Eric laughed. "Point taken."

"You know," said Rohan, looking up at the sky, "I can't help wondering what it must've been like for them. For the original Supers, I mean. If Plunkett was telling the truth, then they could do almost anything. . . ."

"Yeah," said Mollie. "They could all stare at moon craters together, then have stink-cloud contests."

"I'm serious," said Rohan. "Flight, strength, invisibility, they could do it all. No limits. It's kind of scary to think about all that power in the hands of a bunch of . . . well, a bunch of kids."

No one said anything for a while after that. The three of them just continued searching for the shooting stars that weren't there, until they saw a car's headlights and the driver honked at them.

"That's my dad," said Rohan. "Come on, Mollie. We can drop you off on the way. You need a ride, Daniel?"

"No thanks," he answered. "My mom's on her way."

"Okay. Well, it's back to house arrest for all of us, I suppose."

"Yeah. Maybe with good behavior, we can get paroled in time for next summer's break," said Mollie, rolling her eyes.

The two of them waved from the car as they drove away, leaving Daniel and Eric alone together on the porch.

"Eric?" Daniel said after a minute. "Have you thought any more about who Rose said she saw? You know, in the cave?"

Eric kept his eyes on the heavens, but Daniel could see the corners of his mouth turn down into a frown. "Yeah. I hope she's lying."

"Why? If Johnny Noble really is still out there . . ."

"Then he's going to have to answer to me! Don't you get it, Daniel? If Johnny Noble exists, then that means that he abandoned us. We were his children, and he ignored us for all these years while some creep like Plunkett preyed on us!"

Daniel was taken aback by the sudden venom in Eric's voice—the hurt. There was an anger in his friend, just under the surface, and it was kind of frightening. But it was over as quickly as it started.

"Sorry," Eric said, gesturing to the house behind him. "I guess I just have a thing with deadbeat deads. Listen, my mom's going to be in there cleaning up for a while. Do you think you could do me one last birthday favor before your parents get here?"

"Sure. What is it?"

"Just keep a lookout," he said with a smile. "Today's my thirteenth birthday and there is something I've just gotta do!"

And with that, Eric stretched out his arms, closed his eyes and slowly lifted off the ground. He reached twenty feet up into the air and just floated there. From where Daniel was, he could see the look on Eric's face—it was pure ecstasy, freedom. It was joy. Then, like a bullet, he disappeared into the night sky.

"Happy birthday, Eric," said Daniel, plunging his hands into his coat pockets and stamping his feet to keep warm. "Happy birthday."

Back in his room, Daniel looked through his telescope one last time before bed.

The stars were bright, but still static. Not a one fell.

Daniel sat back and glanced over at the old photograph that he now had framed on his desk. In the picture were the original survivors of the St. Alban's fire—just a few of the countless unwanted orphans from around the world, suddenly made special. There was Gram, and Daniel had spotted Mollie's great-grandmother in the crowd. Rohan and Eric, Clay and Bud, Louisa and Rose and Michael and so many others had descended from those scared, lonely few. Daniel felt sad for them, for all of them—even Herman. They'd had no idea what was in store for them; they were only children after all.

Daniel let his gaze drift over to the lights across the street. The Lees were probably going through their usual routines, oblivious to the remarkable daughter who had shown so much bravery in the face of so much fear. He knew that they loved their little girl, but he thought it a shame that they didn't know—*couldn't* know—what a hero she really was.

Daniel's eye was drawn to the streetlight near the edge

of his yard. A man was standing there, looking up at Daniel's window. It was the well-dressed man he'd met outside Plunkett's house—the one who'd come to the house after Gram's funeral—and he was smiling a big, bearded smile. He gave Daniel a small wave. . . . And like that, he was gone. In a blink, Daniel was looking at an empty street where the only movement was the slight stirring of the leaves.

Daniel looked back at the photo, and this time he ignored the frightened faces of the children and focused instead on their savior, Johnny himself. The man in the photo was filthy, and sixty years younger—but Daniel knew him. He was sure of it. He remembered Rose's message, the one delivered by the mysterious stranger who'd been watching them all along—*there are more answers out there, for a good detective to find.*

Daniel stayed at his window for a long while, but nothing more happened. Johnny never reappeared. It was just an empty street.

He was in the bathroom brushing his teeth when he heard Georgie pounding on the door.

"My turn," he was saying from out in the hallway. "My turn!" Georgie was speaking in small sentences now, which elicited an increasingly excited (and annoying) kind of enthusiasm from their parents.

"No, Georgie," Daniel called through a mouthful of toothpaste. "Wait your turn. Wait your turn!"

Daniel saw the doorknob begin to twist, so he reached

over and quickly pushed the lock on the door handle. The knob jiggled with Georgie's frustration.

Pleased with himself, Daniel turned back to spit in the sink when he heard a sharp crack, followed by the squeak of the door swinging open. Daniel turned to see Georgie standing in the open doorway, the doorknob clutched tightly in his hand.

"My turn," he said.

Georgie had pulled the handle, lock and all, out of the door. He had ripped the doorknob off the door. . . .

"No way!" gasped Daniel. "No way."

"Georgie?" came their father's voice from down the hall. "What are you doing? Oh brother!"

Their father appeared next to the diapered tot and took the dismembered doorknob out of his hand. "I thought I fixed this! The wooden door has warped, and now the darn handle keeps falling right out of the frame. Oh well. Looks like we'll just have to knock for a while. Daniel, are you all right? You look a little pale, son. . . ."

Daniel couldn't sleep. As always, there were questions that kept him awake. What would happen next? Daniel was proud of what he'd done for the Supers of Noble's Green; he was glad that they had their futures back. But he also had a secret, a small fear that he could never share with them, with his friends who meant so much.

He threw back his blankets, padded softly across the floor and pulled down a book from the tallest shelf.

It was a special copy of the Sherlock Holmes story *The Final Problem,* which he set on his desk.

The world was going to change, and Daniel knew it. Maybe not tomorrow, maybe not next month or even next year, but it would change. Eric, Mollie, Rohan, Louisa and even Rose were going to get older. They were going to grow up. So would Clay and Bud. And who knew who else? There might be children yet to discover, with powers yet to be explained. The Shroud would no longer threaten them, but over the years he had also used his fortune to help keep them a secret. Now that he was gone, how long would it be before the world discovered that there were genuine superheroes? And what would the Supers do in return?

And then there was Plunkett's warning about the comet, the fire from the sky, the Witch Fire. . . .

It's coming back. And when it does, we must be ready.

He remembered the paintings in Plunkett's cave, the warnings left by a dead civilization. That was why Daniel kept the book on his top shelf—a special book with hollowed-out pages to hide its secret . . . a dark and terrible thing.

Daniel opened the front cover and there, in a small space cut out of the very pages, was a ring. A small, innocent-looking ring of polished stone that no one knew about and, Daniel prayed, no one would ever have to use.

Daniel's attention was drawn again to the window, by a flicker of light and a quick movement in the corner of his vision. He peered through the glass and smiled. Then he placed the book (and its secret) back on its shelf.

He carefully dragged his desk chair over to the window and sat down, propping his head in his hands. The street was still empty, but the sky was full of streaks of trailing fire. The shooting stars were golden, though, not green. It was just an ordinary meteor shower, and it lit the heavens over Mount Noble.

Acknowledgments

There are a lot of people to thank and I'm afraid I'll leave out a few. Thanks to the wonderful writers of the Fantastic Saloon—both past and present. Thanks to James Bessoir for the constant reminder of how fun it is to be a boy. Thanks to Keyan Bowes for conversations on research and to Allison Wortche for her thoughtful edits. To my agent, Kate Schafer Testerman, for believing in me in the first place and being an all-around great friend, and to my editor, Joan Slattery, for giving me the chance and guiding me along the way.

About the Author

Matthew Cody divides his time between writing and teaching college English in New York City. *Powerless,* his first novel, comes from a lifelong love of superhero comics and 1940s pulp fiction.

Originally from the Midwest, Matthew lives with his wife and young son in Manhattan, where he's at work on his next novel for Knopf. You can visit him on the Web at www.matthewcody.com.